for Lisa,
always

OUR WONDERFUL SISTER STATE

I'm the guy who pumps your gas.

Oregon is one of only two states where it's illegal to pump your own gas. The other is New Jersey. Go figure. Great company for us.

It's not horrible working at Buy-Rite. I guess. It's too bad it's not one of the good stations, like Shell or something where I could really be selling out.

Our uniforms are gray, with a thick black horizontal stripe in the middle. Ugly as shit. Either way it's a job and the only one I could get. Restaurants wouldn't even hire me to wash dishes, like the stench of being kicked out of college emanates from my person.

A car rolls in, the bell dings. "What can I do for you?" It's the same old game. Fill it up with regular. Mid-grade. Premium.

Today gas went over two dollars.

You can bet we'll hear about it.

"What the hell's with gas prices?"

"$2.05, are you kidding?"

"Are prices this high because you're pumping it for me?"

And those are the polite ones. I follow my boss' lead, "Fire at a refinery in Washington. It's driving prices up all over the west coast."

Craig, my boss, is selling cigarettes to a guy with a crew cut and a muscle-tee. "When I was in 'Nam," he says. I don't listen to the rest. I finish washing the customer's windshield. When the car leaves I go back in the office and wait for roided-out G.I.Joe to make his exit.

"No way you were in Vietnam," I say, and Craig shoots me a bug-eyed look.

"Of course I was."

"You're forty-two, right?"

Craig nods.

"You were too young to be in Vietnam." He doesn't give in.

"How the hell would you know, kid?"

"I was a history minor."

"Before you got the boot you mean."

Oh, the knife in the side. "Yes," I say. "Regardless, you were too young to be in Vietnam."

"You don't know what I've seen," he says. "Gooks everywhere. I laid in trenches for days in the mud."

I can't help laughing. "Maybe the trenches of your backyard."

ASHLAND

No one wants to live in the town where they grew up. No one wants to leave then come back. Getting kicked out of school didn't give me much choice.

Ashland is a town of contrasts. There are retirees and college kids. Hippies and rich right-wingers. It's yuppie and pretentious, down to earth and artsy. There aren't many places like it in Oregon, just Eugene and Portland. They are the three deposits of culture spread out across the state.

Ashland is nice. But that's all.

It has a Shakespeare festival and a tourist season from hell. It has naked protestors and old people driving Beamers.

After getting kicked out, I didn't know what to do but go back home.

I'll kick myself forever if I get stuck here.

TOURETTE'S

Right now there are only three of us working at the station. Craig, me and this girl, Quinn. She's half-deaf but doesn't like to wear her hearing aid. Sometimes when she's standing next to the pumps she doesn't hear a car driving up behind her.

And she's obsessed with Nirvana.

"Nirvana's watered-down crap," I say when she's working a swing-shift that overlaps with mine. She looks like she might cry. I don't stop. "They were the most sugar-coated butt cheese to come out of the grunge era, which is why they had so much mass-appeal."

"Kurt Cobain was a god," she says.

"Kurt Cobain was the least talented person in that shitty band. Even other musicians in the grunge scene were shocked when Nirvana got signed. They thought of Cobain as a retarded younger brother, who they humored."

Quinn takes *In Utero* out of the stereo and returns it to her backpack.

It's five, which means Quinn should be leaving. I'm here until nine, when we close. But she hasn't left. We haven't had a customer in an hour and neither of us has said a word. She's just standing there at the dingy, fake marble countertop.

"Want me to blow you?" she says. Doesn't even look up when she says it.

Even with all the abuse. Or maybe because of it.

I can't look at her. "No," I say, shaking my head. I walk out of the office into the ninety degree evening. Not laughing. Not laughing, but wanting to.

Quinn swings her backpack onto her shoulder, doesn't bother clocking out, just starts down the street. She's got her headphones on. Right now she's probably listening to "Smells Like Teen Spirit" and thinking about cutting herself. But she's got "chickens out" written all over her.

The next time I see Quinn she tells me she's going to get me fired. That's the first minute of my shift. We've got four hours and fifty-nine minutes left of working together. She's got the closing shift this time, because Craig gave me the weekend off. I'm just filling in for the peak hours.

She stands in the office while I take care of every car that comes in. "Think you might want to help a bit?" I ask and she shakes her head. I'm checking a car's oil when she screams, "You fucking rat bastard!"

I pretend I didn't hear it. The customer, standing next to me as I wipe the dipstick off with a towel, looks at me like I should have an explanation. "Tourette's," I say, which gets rid of the staring.

When there's finally a moment without any cars, I go in the office. "It'd be nice if you decided to do some work today."

"Asshole," she says.

"I'm sorry. Are you mad I wouldn't let you suck my dick." I can't help myself.

The bell rings. "What can I do for you today?" I put on my charmer grin and pump the gas.

Quinn gets on her cell phone and starts pacing around the office.

Three more cars pull in.

I walk into the office and clock out. "If you think this is a one person job today, you can have it."

She stares at me.

The pumps are now backed up with two more cars. "Have fun," I say.

I call Craig while I walk to my car. Tell him I left work. "You did what?" he says.

"Quinn was sitting around on her cell phone while I hustled my ass off. So I left. Let her do some work."

"Did you fuck her?"

"No. Ironically that's the problem."

Craig lets out a sigh. "She thinks she's going to get me fired," I say. "I'm not going to fire you," he says. "But leaving was unprofessional."

Fuck that. "I'd had it with her shit. She was yelling obscenities at me in front of customers."

"Shit," Craig says. "I'll see you on Monday." But he calls me the next day. Wants to talk to Quinn and me. When I get there she's already in the office red-faced and yelling. I hear her before I even get to the door.

"If you don't fire him, I'll quit," she says. I can't keep from smiling. Craig would never admit it, but I know he wouldn't dream of firing me. I'm the first reliable employee he's had since he took over as manager. He's said it a thousand times.

"I'm not going to fire him."

Quinn flips Craig off and walks out the door. Sticks her tongue out at me on her way past.

"Want me to take her shifts?" I ask when Craig comes out of the office. He shakes his head. "I got it. You go have your weekend. I'll see you Monday."

PROMOTION

Less than a month on the job and I'm promoted to Assistant Manager. I get a five-cent raise, crappier shifts and become responsible for things like doing the books at the end of the night, or making deposits. I get the combination to the safe. Craig tells me not to take these things lightly.

Quinn's been replaced by a hippie with hair down to his ass. His name's Mikael, but I call him, "Hair." So far he hasn't seemed to have a problem with it.

Business has slowed because it's the end of summer. By six o'clock the station's pretty much dead. A car every twenty minutes or so. Less. An ancient Oldsmobile pulls in and the old lady driving asks me to check her oil. I force my best work grin. "Of course."

The hydraulics on the hood's lift are shot, so it wobbles like it's going to fall at any moment. And it does. Right when I've got my head all the way in there, trying to shove the dipstick back in its slot on the side of the engine. The hood crashes down, right on the top of my head. Knocks me to the ground.

"Are you all right," the old lady says. Doesn't even bother to get out of the car. "Your oil looks great," I say. She thanks me and drives off. I go around the side of the office and puke on the sidewalk.

I get out the hose and wash down the concrete. I puke three more times.

At closing time I'm shutting down and I slip on the wet and soapy cement. I hit my head again. "Fuck," I say, then repeat it a few times for good measure. When I stand up I puke again, but it's all dry heaves at this point.

When I get back to my parent's house, which I'm house-sitting while they're camping, I call my brother. "Sounds like a concussion," he says. "Stay there and I'll pick you up."

"I'm already home," I say.

"What? You shouldn't be driving with a concussion."

"It was fine. I listened to Led Zeppelin's *II*, I was fine."

"You're an idiot," my brother says.

CLOSING

I'm closing up the station. Shutting down, locking the bathroom and storeroom doors, padlocking all the pumps. Getting ready to do a quick cigarette count and speed through the paperwork so I can get home.

I see them approaching from a block away—these two girls and I know they're coming here. They don't look they're from around here.

One girl's in a black tank-top, a red plaid schoolgirl skirt, and black boots up to her knees. The other's wearing tight cutoff-jean shorts and a white T-shirt.

"Do you have a bathroom?" the one in cutoff-shorts says.

"Sure. I'll unlock it for you."

"Thank you so much," the one in the skirt says.

Both girls go into the single stall bathroom. I pull the hose in from next to the vacuums. The door to the bathroom is partially open. I should close it, I think.

Or maybe they want me to walk in? The idea is like something out of a porn movie, but I can't help thinking it.

I lock the office door. They are still in the bathroom, the door's still ajar. I hear them giggling. I can't stop myself, I push it open.

"Sorry," I say, ready to defend myself. The girls are standing there laughing. The one in the skirt is kissing the other's neck. She grabs my hand and pulls me in. The one in cutoff-shorts locks the door.

Skirt unzips my Buy-Rite issued gray slacks. Cutoff-shorts pulls her T-shirt over her head, drops her shorts to the floor that I didn't sweep before locking up. Soon they're both naked and my thing's hanging out of my underwear. They take turns touching it, putting it in their mouths. They kiss. I touch their tits. And they finger each other, their shaved parts looking like bald twins.

When they finish me off, Skirt smacking her lips with a sly grin, I tuck myself back in and pull up my pants. I watch them dress. No one's said a word since I opened the door. That doesn't change until they are walking out of the bathroom, when Skirt turns and blows me a kiss.

"Thanks again," she says.

And the door closes.

BIRTHDAY

Craig is giving me three days off. Tomorrow is my twenty-first birthday. He said he wants to make sure I'm sober by the time I come back to work. It's Thursday so I get a real three-day weekend. He leaves work at one as usual, but pulls back into the station thirty minutes later, hands me a heavy brown paper bag.

"Don't use any of that until you leave work," he says. Then he tells me happy birthday and sputters off in his twenty-five year old pickup.

The bag is full of liquor. All sorts of shit. Like he went into the liquor store and asked for a grab bag of their worst selling products. Maybe he's just got shit taste in booze.

I'm house-sitting for my parents, again and when I get home from work I open Craig's bag. I close my eyes and reach in. The bottle I pull out is peach vodka. I twist off the cap, throw it in the trash and slump into the couch. I turn the TV on and tip the bottle into the air, pouring the foulest tasting shit into my throat.

At midnight I finish off the bottle and go to the stereo. I blast The Beatles' "Birthday" and sing along. This should be a tradition, I think. Then I flop onto the couch, try not to puke and pass out.

Carey, a friend of mine from college, drives down for my birthday. He gets in around dinner and we order a pizza, washing it down with whatever we pull out of the Craig's magic bag of booze. He's not twenty-one yet, so we stay in all night watching movies like *Bubba Ho-Tep* and *Boondock Saints* while getting blitzed. The next morning he gets back in his car to drive the five hours back to school.

Saturday night my brother and I hit the bars. I drink Long Island Iced-Teas everywhere we stop. At one bar my brother hits the dance floor and this older guy sits next to me at the bar. "You look familiar," he says.

"I work at a gas station," I say. "I probably look familiar to half the people in this bar."

The man smiles and it dawns on me that he's flirting.

"I own a retro clothing store," he says.

I nod.

"You should come in some time."

"Retro's cool. But I work at a gas station and that means no money," I say, shrugging my shoulders and hoping he'll take a hint, leave me alone.

"Who said anything about needing money," he says, and that's when I lose it. I kick my stool out from under me like a badass in an action movie.

"Back off, man. I'm not going to come to your store, and I'm definitely not going to let you perv out on me. Freak."

Everybody in the bar is looking.

The guy doesn't look embarrassed. Sadly it's probably not the first time this has happened to him.

My brother drives me home. I walk inside with a singular purpose: to brush my teeth, my personal yardstick for whether or not I'm too drunk.

It's cold when I wake up. I open my eyes and see the base of the toilet. My toothbrush is in my mouth and I'm naked. I get to my knees and dump my toothbrush in the sink. Then I crawl to the couch and fall back asleep.

FIRED

Hair and his wife have been stealing cigarettes. It took me a few weeks to figure it out. Every other Sunday his shift comes up five packs of Gold 100's short. It didn't really hit me until his wife asked for a pack when she came to pick up his paycheck. So I staked out the store one Sunday and watched her grab the packs from the shelf and toss them on the front seat of their pickup.

When I told Craig he said, "Fuck." He didn't want to fire Hair because Hair has three kids and one of them has two of her own. And they all live with Hair. And his wife looks like a meth addict. And as if that's not enough problems for one guy to have, Craig knows no one else is going to hire Hair.

But he has to fire him.

"You want to do it?" Craig asks.

I shrug, say, "Sure." I don't have anything against the guy other than he's kind of an idiot, but I also don't have sympathy for someone who steals shitty cigarettes for their crack whore-looking wife.

So Craig calls Hair. Calling him Mikael, of course and asks him to come down to the station. When he shows up Craig goes to the bathroom. Doesn't want to be anywhere nearby when I drop the bomb.

"What's up?" Hair asks.

I say, "Mikael you're fired." Flat out like that. No fucking around. He looks at me with a blank stare, so I press on. "I know you and your wife are stealing cigarettes. It didn't take that long to figure out where we were coming up short every other Sunday. Then I saw it happen with my own eyes. As much as Craig likes you, you can't keep paying a person to steal from you."

"It's because I won't cut my hair, isn't it?"

"No, Mikael, it's because you were stealing cigarettes."

He gets into his truck. "That's discrimination," he says, leaning out the window.

For a second I wonder if he's talking about the stealing.

CHANGES

Rumors are swirling. Big changes headed our way. The suits from our parent company are visiting the station on a near-daily basis. They shake my hand like it's the lever on a slot machine. They say things like, "We want to take this station to the next level."

They put in a new, "state-of-the-art" car wash. Craig takes a vacation and leaves me working five full days in a row. Right when they're installing the damn thing. It's his way of showing he doesn't like the changes that are being made. I end up putting in five days of over sixteen hours, because the guy installing the car wash always holds me up explaining how the damn thing works.

The suits say things like, "When it's up and running that wash is going to bring in piles of cash."

Craig says if they really want to make money they ought to make it a topless car wash. He's probably closer to being right.

There are four wash options. The top of the line is ten bucks. For a car wash.

"People will line up for the deluxe wash," the suits say. "It's all about quality."

They're so out of touch they don't realize it's only about quality if it's quality at a bargain. Other than that it's about cheap, cheap, cheap.

CIGARETTES

Some teenagers come in and try to buy cigarettes. They cuss under their breath when I card them. One backs up to the door and lets out a nervous chuckle.

"I wasn't trying to buy any," he says. "I told you guys it wouldn't work."

The next day I see the same kids across the street from the station talking to an older guy who's walking past. They hand him some cash and he crosses the street.

"Three packs of Camels," he says when he comes into the office.

I laugh. "Sorry man, I saw them give you the money. I can't sell cigarettes to you, I know they're for minors."

"No sweat off my sack," he says and walks out the door.

Across the street one of the kids gives me the finger and another yells "asshole."

A girl comes into the station one day and asks for a pack of Parliaments. I ask for her ID and she lifts her shirt. Her breasts are pale white, a few freckles scattered across them. Her nipples are hard and brown.

"Parliaments?" I say.

She nods and smiles, pulls her shirt back down.

One of my regular customers comes in every other day for six packs of Marlboro Reds. He works three jobs and pops in for smokes on his way from one to the next. And with each purchase he tells me a dirty joke.

Some are simple, like "What do you call someone who sucks dick? Cock Breath." But some are incredibly complex and require diagrams and pictures on scraps of paper.

He even comes in for cigarettes after his wedding. His new wife is in the car and so are her two teenage kids. They get gas and he asks for six packs of Marlboro Reds and six Camel Lights for his wife. He doesn't tell me a joke this time, but I tell him and his wife congratulations and they grin like middle-aged idiots. One of the teenagers is on a cell phone, and the other is running her fingers through her hair.

A kid—probably younger than me, comes in one evening an hour before closing. He pulls a pocketknife out and points it at me. He's as tall as me, but scrawny. I think I see his hand shaking.

"Give me all the money in the register," he says.

I look him dead on. "You really want to do this?"

We stand there for a good minute or more. Him holding the knife in the air, me with my hands at my side.

"No," he says, and folds the blade back into the handle "Give me a pack of American Spirit Blues," he says and pulls a five-dollar bill from his pocket.

CODE FOR FAILURE

I'm pumping gas for a guy in a light blue polo shirt one day when he says, "I used to work here. About five years ago."

"Oh yeah?" I say, knowing full well that working at a gas station's not really code for anything, except maybe failure.

"Don't ever get comfortable here," he says. "This place will steal your soul."

I smile. The woman in the front seat of his car is re-applying her lipstick.

"I'm not kidding," he says.

I nod.

"This place will fucking steal your soul." The man says it one more time as he gets back in his car.

I can't help but wonder what he does for work now that he's not pumping gas.

GINGER

A glimmering black BMW pulls in one night, when there haven't been any customers for hours. "What can I do for you?" Fill with premium. The guy in the passenger seat puts a magazine on his lap and dumps a pile of white powder on it. Starts sifting it into lines.

"What are you doing?" the driver says.

"Just doing a couple lines before the party."

The driver smacks his passenger in the back of the head. "What if this guy's a cop," he says, jabbing his thumb in my direction.

"Don't worry about me," I say.

"See?" the passenger says. "I knew he was cool."

"You cool?" the driver asks, giving me a half-nod.

"The coolest. That'll be twenty-three fifty."

The driver pulls a fifty off a roll of bills. "Keep the change," he says. "And if you're looking for a party tonight, we'll be on Tolman Creek. You won't be able to miss it."

"I don't close until nine."

"No party's good until after ten anyway," he says, rolling up his window.

After work I figure I've got nothing to lose and drive up Tolman Creek Road looking for the party. Almost at the end of the road there's a big house lit up like someone's afraid of the dark. There are eight cars in the driveway, including the Beamer. I take off my work shirt and decide my white T-shirt underneath will have to be good enough. There's no point knocking so I just walk right into the house.

The party's not exactly raging. There are a few people draped over the furniture in the living room, bottles in their hands. In the kitchen there's a small crowd of people who can still stand. On the back patio I find the guys from the Beamer. They greet me like it was expected that I would show.

"Someone cut this guy a line," the driver says.

Someone else hands me a bottle of Wild Turkey. I take a tug, holding my mouth tight to keep from grimacing. Wild Turkey is the nastiest shit. The passenger from the Beamer puts out a line on the rail of the patio and presents it to me with a sweep of his hand. I hold one finger to the side of my nose and snort. I swear I can smell the coat of varnish on the railing. And a brief hint of cedar.

I end up on a couch next to a petite redhead. She's talking a million miles an hour and I'm nodding my head saying, "uh huh."

I have to piss. Like now. But she never gives an inch for me to cut in. Finally I'm going to burst. "I really like talking to you," I say. "But I've got to piss like crazy."

"That's cool," she says. "I'll come. I need to pee, too."

I think she means she'll wait outside. Go after me. But apparently that's not what she had in mind, because she follows me into the bathroom. If I didn't have to go so bad I would never be able to do it with her standing next to me.

"Don't worry," she says. "I won't look." But I can feel her eyes peering over my shoulder.

When I'm finished she shoves her jeans down to her ankles. I turn my head out of instinct while she pees. She pulls her pants back up.

"Do you have a credit card?" she asks.

I don't even think twice, just pull it out my wallet. She takes the card and pulls a plastic bag from her pocket. She chops out a line on the back lid of the toilet and vacuums it with her nose. She hands the card back to me and I slide it in my wallet.

She stands and presses herself against me, kisses me like she's never done it before, or has forgotten how. Her lips push hard against mine, making my teeth ache. She unbuttons her pants again. This time I don't turn away. Her underwear is like the kind a kid would wear. White with cartoon dinosaurs on it. She pushes those down her slender milk-white thighs, too.

Her copper pubic hair catches what light there is in the bathroom until she hits the lights and everything goes dark. She pulls my pants down and I pick her up, slide in. I stumble forward, until I'm pressing her against the wall.

She gyrates herself up and down at a frantic, almost hypnotic pace.

She squeaks like a mouse and her body goes limp. A couple more thrusts and I finish, too.

She doesn't bother to pull up her pants or even her underwear, just asks if she can use my credit card again. I bend over to pull it out of my pants, still shrugged around my feet.

Two more lines snorted and she doesn't bother offering any to me. But I'm still buzzing from the Wild Turkey, which is probably what made me have to pee so bad in the first place. Then she's on me again. I'm surprised to find myself able

"I'm going to call you Ginger," I say when she squeaks and all her muscles relax into my arms, like liquid.

She laughs. "Okay," she says.

INK

When Craig leaves, I put the Misfits' *Walk Among Us* on. We're supposed to have "neutral" music on. If any. But to Craig that means the country or gospel radio stations and I can't take that crap.

It's a slow day and I'm singing along, when somebody walks in the office and clears their throat. I look up and play it off.

"What can I do for you?"

The guy's forest service green SUV is parked outside.

"American Spirit Yellows," he says.

I pull a pack from the shelf.

"Danzig or Jerry Only?" he asks.

"Danzig. Always. You can't beat his voice."

He nods. His arms are covered in tattoos of Dali paintings.

"Who does your ink?"

"I did most of them," he says.

"No shit? I've been looking for someone new. The guy who did my last one fucked it up." I peel up my sleeve to exhibit the botched tree of life on my bicep.

"I can fix that," he says. "Name's Davis." He hands me a business card. "That's got my number on it. Right now I'm working out of my apartment, but if you're cool with that we can totally set something up."

"I've got the next two days off. Any chance you can do it tonight?"

"What time you get off work?"

"Nine."

"Sure." He starts scribbling his address on a scrap of paper. "What do you want to get done?"

I dig in my backpack and pull out a drawing of a nautical star. "This," I say handing it to him.

"Got it," he says. "See you after nine."

After my shift, I start my car and the Ramones blast out through the speakers. I always forget to turn down the volume before I get out of my car. I scream along. All the way to Davis' apartment.

He's outside stubbing out a cigarette when I pull up to the curb.

"You ready?" he asks.

"You know it."

It's been six months since my last tattoo. Somehow over time you forget what it feels like when the needle vibrates through the pores of your skin.

Davis wipes the excess ink away as he goes. I'm laying on my side in a reclined La-Z-Boy in his spare bedroom. My palms sweat with each line. Even though the needle is being worked into the side of my calf the pain feels like the skin behind my knee is being pinched.

We take a break so Davis can smoke.

In another twenty minutes he's done.

"Want me to wrap it up?" he asks.

I shrug. "No need."

"Going bare like a fucking rock star," he says, and I hand him a hundred dollar bill.

"Quite a deal," I say.

He gives me a nod. "Any time, man."

HOW I GOT KICKED OUT OF SCHOOL

"So," Craig says when we're both waiting for tanks to fill, "what got you kicked out of college, anyway?"

"Drinking," I say and the guy in the Corolla whose gas I'm pumping looks at me in the rear-view mirror. When the customers leave I finish the story. "I used to walk through the halls of my dorm carrying a half-gallon of rum. I got written up a lot and eventually they asked me to go the school's therapist and AA meetings."

Craig draws the end of one cigarette and uses the butt to light another.

"I told the dean to screw herself."

Craig cracks a smile "You can't tell me this is better than being at school."

"It's not," I say. "I don't really like people telling me what to do. I'm not going to pump gas forever."

"You better not," he says. "I won't wait for booze to do the job, I'll kill you myself." He scrunches his face and bugs out his eyes, looking at me with his head cocked to the side. "I was in 'Nam, bitch."

SECOND JOB

A silver-haired real estate agent pulls into the station in a light blue convertible Mustang. She's in every other week. After filling her tank, she signs her credit card slip, then hands me her business card.

"I'll pay you $500 dollars to keep me company tonight," she says.

I don't know how to respond.

"I wrote my home number on the back of the card."

"I'm not off until nine."

"You call me you won't be off until breakfast," she says and winks.

I set the card on the counter in the office. $500 dollars is more than I make in two weeks of pumping gas. And she's not bad looking. For an older lady. I mean, she's fit. She wears tighter clothes than most twenty-year olds. But she's at least in her mid-fifties. If not older.

When I close the station I call from my cell phone. She says, "Hello," and I say, "I'm in." She tells me how to get to her house.

The house is huge. Her mustang is parked in the middle of the arching driveway. I park behind it. She answers the door in an evening gown. Like we're attending some high society event in a Carey Grant movie.

"My husband's away on business," she says. "He's always sleeping around. I figure I might as well have some fun, too."

"Can I get you a drink?" she asks.

"I could really use a shower," I say. "I came straight from work."

She shows me upstairs to her shower and leaves to make me a Jack and Coke. Her bathroom is bigger than my whole apartment.

The towels are monogrammed. SM and AM. I use the AM, figuring it's her husband's since her name is Sondra. She comes in while I'm drying off and doesn't miss a beat, just hands me a glass.

"Looks like I made a good choice," she says. She pulls a robe from a hook by the bathroom door and hands it to me. "No point in getting dressed again."

Her purse is sitting on the dresser opposite her bed and she reaches in, pulls out a folded wad of bills, hands it to me.

"Five," she says. "Like we agreed." As if there was some sort of contract in place.

"That's a lot of money," I say. "For what? A night of fucking?"

"When you get my age," she says, "certain things become more valuable. Like young men and long nights." She turns her back to me. "Unzip me?"

I do and she slinks out of the gown. Her stomach is flat and her ass curves under the lines of her black panties in a way that would never betray her age.

"You won't mind if I leave the bra on?" she asks. "The one part of time I haven't been able to combat." Her bra holds her breasts erect like she's just blossomed.

I shake my head.

In the morning she brings me a cup of coffee.

"I have to work," I say.

"Me, too," she says.

ON THE RISE

Prices are still on the rise. Just enough to keep people complaining.

"Not like I see any of it on my paycheck," I say. I'm making twenty cents over minimum wage. Not exactly an oil tycoon.

Craig sums up the obvious, "The oil industry is fucked."

But nothing keeps customers from taking it out on us.

A guy fills up his oversized pickup, jacked up higher than most monster trucks. Compensation? Probably. Filling both tanks the total comes to a hundred dollars even.

"What the fuck?" he says when I tell him. Like it's my fault he has an inferiority complex. If he could come to terms with it and buy a compact he wouldn't have this problem. But I don't say that. It wouldn't do any good.

Then, to top it off the guy's credit card is declined.

"You can park over there," I say pointing to the two spots next to the office. "There are three banks in the area, so you can get cash."

"I'm not paying. Fuck that."

He's the real articulate type. He starts his engine. I peek around the back of the truck.

"Well," I say, "I just memorized your license plate number, so I'll be giving the police a call."

His face turns a few shades of purple and he steps down from the truck. Starts walking across the street. Like a true prick he leaves the truck where it is, holding up three cars behind him. All of who back out and drive away to another station.

He comes back and throws a hundred dollar bill at me. It flutters to the ground halfway between us. It kicks up again when he drives off. I pick it up.

I think it's safe to say he won't be a repeat customer.

JIHAD

Every day Craig pulls out a pair of binoculars to spy on the Chevron station a block up the street from us. We're told to match their prices and they know it. Sometimes they change their prices three times in one day, to make us scramble.

But today, before Craig can take the binoculars out of their black plastic case Steve Selway, the manager of the Chevron walks into the office.

"They're selling the station," Selway says.

"No shit?" Craig says, barely looking up from the cigarette order he's pretending to fill.

"To some fucking Muslims," Selway says.

"The ones who own the Chevron on the other side of town?"

"Yeah. And there's no way I'm working for some towel-head terrorist family."

"I'm not sure they qualify as terrorists," I say.

Selway ignores me. "Isn't it good enough that they control our oil supply? Now they want our gas stations, too?"

"First off, just because they're from the Middle East doesn't mean they have any stake in the oil there," I say.

"This is how they're going to infiltrate," Selway says.

"How many packs of Parliaments do we have?" Craig asks.

"Making a damn sleeper cell out of my gas station."

"Six," I say holding up my fingers in Craig's direction. "Secondly, just because they're Muslim doesn't mean they're terrorists."

Selway slams his hand on the counter. "You better watch out, Craig," he says. "Looks like you've got a communist in your employ." He jabs his finger in the air at me and storms out of the office.

"Aiaiaiaiaiai." Selway howls all the way up the street.

JOE DIRT

"You know the best movie ever?" Craig asks.

"*Citizen Kane*?" I say.

He shakes his head. "*Joe Dirt*. Funniest movie you'll ever see."

"With David Spade?"

"Yeah. He plays a total hick. It's hilarious."

"You know," I say. "You kind of look like David Spade."

"Sweet," Craig says.

"And by that I mean, you look like an old weasel that resembles David Spade."

"Lick my butt hole."

"You're sick," I say.

Then the bell dings.

"What can I do for you?" Five, Ten, Twenty of regular.

NEW NAME

When I show up to work all the signs have been changed. The Buy-Rite signs are gone. Everything is Texaco. Two days off and we're a new station.

Did the station get sold? Do I have a job?

Seeing Craig when I walk up to the office calms my nerves. "What the hell happened?" I ask.

Craig laughs. "Confused?"

"Just a bit," I say.

Turns out ownership hasn't changed. Just our "branding."

"We going to get new uniforms?" I ask and Craig says, "No."

Damn.

"Didn't Shell take Texaco over?"

"Did they?" Craig asks.

"I heard they were phazing the Texaco name out because they had a history of racist hiring practices."

"Huh."

All day customers ask if we've got new owners. They ask if the change is why our prices have gone up. I no longer know what to tell them.

"We're as clueless as you," I say. "Our prices change because someone in an office somewhere calls us and says, 'Put regular at $2.25, mid at $2.35, and premium at $2.45.'" They don't care. All that matters is what used to cost them less than twenty dollars now costs almost thirty. Or more.

"We drive cars, too," I say.

"Do you buy your gas here?" One customer asks.

"Most of the time," I say. But even that's probably more about proximity than anything.

The company that owns our station also owns a Shell station on the other side of town. They've introduced their "V Power" which is supposedly an additive. But our gas comes from the same truck as theirs. And I know enough to know it's the same damn gas.

Ours is three cents cheaper. Sure it's about location, but it's also about the name power, the corporate credibility. Fake as it is.

I tell customers.

"Our gas is the same as theirs. V Power my ass."

I ask myself what good it does. It doesn't get us more customers. I don't even want more customers. Maybe it's the thrill of subversion. Undermining the corporate bullshit.

But I'm not undermining a damn thing. People will keep buying gas they believe is better for their car, or they won't. That's decided by things like economics. Not knowledge.

If I was really concerned with bringing down the hypocrisy of the oil industry I suppose I'd put some active effort into the process. Flyers. Protests. Whatever.

Instead I pump the gas. Whether it's Buy-Rite, Texaco, Chevron, Shell, or any other company my job doesn't change.

MAN-WHORE

Housewives love me. I fill up the tanks of their minivans and they hang out the window, pouting their lips and flirting with me like we're in high school. I can't say I discourage it.

I've been thinking a lot about the whole thing with silver haired Sondra. I tell Craig I'm thinking about having sex for money.

"Brilliant," he says.

"Gas station attendant's a perfect cover, I think."

He agrees.

I think about it every time a housewife flirts with me.

There's no telling exactly what snaps inside me. What makes me do it. But I'm filling the tank of a Dodge minivan. The customer's a regular. Brunette, with an enormous chest that she sets on the window when she talks to me. Today her kids aren't in the car. I've never seen her husband.

Today I check her ring finger. It's there, so she's not divorced.

In the office I run her credit card. While it processes, I write a note on a scrap of paper. "If you'd like some 'companionship' call me." While the receipt prints I debate whether I'll give it to her. The copy of the receipt prints. I hold her copy in one hand with the note.

After she signs the station's copy, I hand hers over.

With the note.

"Have a good evening," I say, flashing a smile Even a hint of a wink.

I can't believe myself.

My palms are sweating. I can't believe I did something so stupid. I could get fired. Although I'm pretty sure Craig would just laugh at me. More than likely she'll just start buying her gas somewhere else.

My cell phone vibrates on the counter.

I don't recognize the number. I never answer my phone when I'm on the clock.

"Hello?"

"I just noticed your note," she says. "When are you free?"

I don't even pause. "Mondays and Tuesdays. Or Wednesday through Sunday night after nine." It flows so easily. Like I'm not myself.

"How about Monday?" she asks. "My husband takes the kids to school at eight, then goes to work. Kids aren't home until a quarter to three. Husband not until six or later."

She's breathing heavy. I bet her hands are clammier than mine.

"Name the time," I say.

"Ten?"

She gives me her address. Asks me how much it will cost.

"Two hundred," I say. Again without a trace of hesitance.

It's Saturday evening. Plenty of time for her to call it off if she chickens out. Same goes for me. But if we don't? I've been called a man-whore before, but in a couple days it could be a lot more than just an insult an ex-girlfriend hurls at me out of spite.

EVERYBODY NEEDS A HAND

After Craig leaves work for the day I try not to call him with any problems that come up. Except for the time the old guy shit all over the floor and walls of the bathroom.

I wasn't about to handle that myself.

So, when the car wash breaks down I decide to fix it myself. The brand new car wash. Already breaking down. There's a gigantic chain, like on a bike, which runs the whole thing. It's hung up on itself.

Tangled. I reach my hand up into the machine and tug on the chain.

No give.

I tug harder.

Nothing.

I put all my weight into it. I'm practically hanging from the damn thing.

It hits me.

I didn't shut the car wash down. If I pull the chain free, it's going to start right back up. The chain's going to start running and my hand is going to be caught in the works.

This, I think, is how people lose hands. Arms. Limbs. Stupid people who don't know better. People who don't put any thought into their actions.

I try to pull my hand free from the chain. My fingers are caught and it starts to move.

I pull on my wrist with my free hand. My shoulder burns from the yanking. The chain gives a little more.

I wonder how much blood there will be. If I will pass out. If they make prosthetic hands. And will it be just like having a real hand?

How long will it take for an ambulance? Will a news van beat them? Are they allowed to show a dismembered hand on TV?

The car wash's motor purrs, and the chain moves two links. Pulls on my fingers. There's one last chance to free my hand before it gets ground up in the mechanics of a state-of-the-art car wash. I jump, tuck my legs under me. My fingers scrape through the links of the chain. It rolls into motion. I land on my knees. Feel it in my spine. My hand is still connected to my wrist. My knuckles are bleeding. My arm aches.

I feel nauseous.

I go to the bathroom. Scrub the dirt, grease and grime from my hand. I ignore the flaps of skin and the blood.

PEOPLE ARE STUPID

"Who the hell steals a vacuum nozzle?" Craig is steaming.

Somebody stole the nozzle fittings off the two vacuums.

"Now we're going to have to take those in at night, too," he says. "What the hell's somebody going to do with those?"

Stealing for the sake of stealing. People would steal the rubber hose for water if we left it out. Anything that can be removed gets locked inside the office at night. Everything.

"It's not like they fit a normal vacuum."

I didn't even know they were removable.

"Teenagers will steal anything," Craig says.

"Idiots will steal anything," I say. "Meth addicts. Drunks. People playing truth and dare."

But really, who steals a vacuum nozzle?

DISPOSABLE

Gas station employees are a disposable commodity.

They come and go. People quit. People get fired. For people under a certain age it's a transitional job. For those over a certain age it's a wasteland, a constant reminder of wrong turns and failures in life.

I don't say that to Craig.

Sometimes I wonder if what happened to him is already happening to me.

At least he hasn't always worked at a gas station. At one time he was a 5-star chef in San Diego. He was married. Had a daughter. Then his wife's coke habit took over. They got divorced. She snorted all the money he'd saved. He lost his job. He took his daughter and moved to Los Angeles, where he drove a limousine. Even drove the Rolling Stones. Still has a roadie's jacket that Mick Jagger gave him.

But that job didn't last either. So he moved his daughter north, to Oregon. Got a job cooking at a small restaurant. Then lost that job, too. Started working at Buy-Rite and in less than six months became the manager of the station.

But this is where I'm starting.

My path to the gas station was a short one. Went to college, got kicked out, got laughed at every place I asked for an application. Except at the gas station, where Craig hired me on the spot.

I've seen the transitional workers. Since firing Hair the Wonder Hippie, we've gone through three employees. All of them younger than me. All of them quitting after a few days or weeks.

Each one making me think I shouldn't be stuck in this job.

Our latest hire is P.J. He's an idiot. He will likely be working at a gas station for the rest of his life, even though he's only eighteen. If you've ever read an *Archie* comic, he's Moose. Or Dauber from that old TV show, *Coach*.

But you can't expect much out of an employee at a gas station. It's a job that goes to former addicts or convicts. High school dropouts. Down and outs.

Believe me, it doesn't make me feel better.

All you can ask is that they show up to work. That they can pump the gas. Or wash a windshield. Is it all I can ask of myself?

There I'm not certain.

DREAMS

"I had a dream last night that I was stuck in the car wash while it was running."

"This job'll get under your skin," Craig says. We're changing the prices on the sign. Up another four cents.

"I hear the bell in my dreams," he says. "Ding, ding, ding. fucking get it."

"That's bad," I say.

"That's when you know you've been doing the job too long."

Craig peers up the street with his binoculars. They haven't screwed around with us since the new owners took over.

"Your dream would have been a lot better if we had a topless car wash, like I suggested," he says.

He's right, it would have.

OFFICE GIRL

We call her Office Girl. Because we don't know anything about her other than she works at an office within walking distance.

And she smokes Camel Lights.

"You've been talking about her since the first time you saw her," Craig says. "Why not gather those brass balls and ask for her number?"

She's coming down the sidewalk for her weekly cigarettes.

"I don't think so," I say.

"Come on," Craig says. He takes a pack of her smokes off the shelf and hands it to me. "Show me some of that smooth talking. Some of that charm you claim to have."

"Hey guys," Office Girl says as she comes in the door.

"Hey," Craig and I say in unison. I can feel the shit-eating grin spreading across my face. My cheeks burning.

Being blonde is a curse. Fair skin gives you away.

Office Girl smiles.

She's wearing a navy knee-length skirt. A white button-up dress shirt, the top three buttons undone. Taunting.

"What were you just saying?" Craig asks, looking at me.

Then he looks to Office Girl. "This guy's got some great stories."

"Oh yeah?" she says. "I'd love to hear one."

I can't think.

What happened to the guy who slipped a soccer mom his number and had sex with her for money?

"But it'll have to be another time," she says.

I breathe.

"The office is crazy today."

I nod. "Another time, then," I say.

She smiles. Takes her cigarettes and change. Waves on her way out the door.

"That's some fatal charm," Craig says, practically slapping his knee he's laughing so hard.

He goes out for a smoke. I follow.

"You could have had her digits," he says. "If you could've talked."

"I froze."

"In the clutch."

"Happens to the best of us," I say.

"Whatever helps you sleep," Craig says, taking a long drag of his Gold Menthol.

NIGHT OFF

Most of my nights off are spent in my studio apartment. I open the windows to get a breeze flowing. I turn on the stereo. Put on the Dead Milkmen. Crank it.

I make spaghetti. Complete with garlic bread. Drink wine straight from the bottle. Thrash my head around to the music while the sauce simmers. I eat in front of the TV. Only get up for more booze, or to take a piss.

Sometimes I get a call from Sondra. Or Catherine, the housewife.

I fall asleep on my futon couch, which I never bother to pull out into a bed.

I leave the dishes in the sink.

But some nights I feel more social and head out to the bars.

Drink rum and cokes, play pool. Tonight there are a couple of girls at the pool table, so I ask if I can play the winner. They look at each other.

"Sure," the blonde in the jean skirt says.

Her name is Seneca. We shake hands.

"You going to win?" I ask.

"Of course," she says, and leans over to line up her next shot.

"While I'm waiting to kick your butt can I buy you a drink?"

"Sure," she says. "Corona."

"And your friend?"

The other girl shakes her head.

"All right, Corona it is."

Seneca does win. Her friend disappears to a booth with a couple of other girls.

"Think you can take me?" Seneca says.

"Not a problem." I wink.

"Is everybody here so friendly?" she asks.

"Not from around here?"

"Just moved."

"In that case, no. I'm the friendliest."

"I see," she says.

"Why'd you move?"

"Just got out of a two-year relationship."

Not the dreaded just got out of a long relationship speech, I think. The, "I'm not ready to move on yet, but my friends dragged me out of the house." We've all heard it.

"I dated this guitarist, and that was crazy. Wanted to start somewhere new."

"Guitarist huh? Would I know the band?"

She breaks. A striped ball goes in the middle left pocket.

"Stripes," she says, then, "The Dead Kennedys."

I know my mouth is hanging open. "You dated East Bay Ray?"

"Yes," she says. "It wasn't really that exciting."

I take my turn. Miss badly. "That's crazy. I can't believe you dated East Bay Ray."

She chuckles. "Take it easy," she says. "Try to focus." She knocks in two more balls. "You're falling behind."

Seneca wins again, I rack up another. Her friends get up from their booth and say they're leaving. She tells them she's going to stay.

Her friends glare at me.

One of them says, "He works at a gas station. I've seen him before."

I pretend not to have heard. Seneca tells them it's okay. That she'll see them later.

I win the third game. "Want to play again?" I ask.

"Why don't we go to my apartment," she says.

I nod. "Definitely better."

Outside her apartment she holds a finger to her lips. "We have to be quiet," she says. "My two-year old is asleep." It's a ballsy time to announce she has a kid. She must know after looking at her bend over the pool table all night I won't ditch out under any circumstances.

Who's babysitting?" I ask.

"My sister," she says. "But don't worry, she's probably asleep on the couch."

She kisses me, pulls my head against hers. Her tongue flicks against my lips. She holds her finger up again.

"Shh," she says, and opens the door.

YELLOW JACKETS

I pop three of them.

A friend turned me onto them when we were studying for a final at the end of our first semester. I haven't been sleeping enough. Drinking too much. Then I come to work. My eyes want to close, but they can't.

It's "What can I do for you?"

It's "fill 'er up."

Bullshit.

I like the striped pills. As if pills need to be decorated. Yellow Jackets. I can't believe you can get this shit over the counter.

I pop three of them. Wash them down with a Red Bull. Then I wait for the customers.

The poor, unsuspecting customers.

DOPE NOSE

A beat up, rusted Cadillac pulls into the station. I get to the window, my "What can I do for you?" poised and ready. But I can't get it out.

The guy in the passenger seat looks like a stereotypical redneck. Mid-eighties mustache, flannel shirt with the sleeves torn off. But what catches me off guard is the driver. A cracked-out looking woman. She's got coke all over the front of her nose and upper lip. Like she was pretending to be a pig searching for truffles when she was snorting lines.

"Five dollars of regular," she says.

"Sure thing," I say, rubbing my nose. Trying to give her a clue. She doesn't get it.

I pump the gas.

I go back to her window. She hands over a plastic bag with quarters in it. "That's five dollars," she says. Normally I'd count it before I let her drive off. But I can't take it any longer.

"You've got a little something on your nose," I say.

All the color, what's left., drains from her face. She looks in the rearview mirror. Rubs her nose with the palm of her hand. She starts the car and drives off without looking at me.

A LESSON

We've got to be the last gas station on the planet without automated pumps. That means if someone wants five dollars of regular we have to stand there while it pumps. For bigger amounts, say twenty dollars, we've got tricks that help a bit. Like sticking a pen under the pump handle so it's held pumping the slightest amount. It allows us to tend to more than one customer at a time.

It's not fool-proof.

The customer has bleach blonde hair. It sticks out from under a zebra-print cowboy hat. It would be too horrid to look at, but she's wearing a pink tube top that she keeps adjusting. She has a wad of ones in her hand and she's digging for change in the ashtray. She counts it up. "$11.85," she says.

"Regular?"

She nods. I use the pen trick, and set to washing her windshield.

"Thanks," she says, hanging her head out the window.

"How's your day going?" I ask.

"Good. Just getting stuff done, you know." She takes off her hat and swishes her hair back and forth. "I'm having such a shitty hair day," she says. "Couldn't leave the house without a hat."

"Your hair looks great," I say. She pulls on the edges of her tube top. I try not to be obvious about looking at her breasts.

"You're sweet," she says.

"Only when someone deserves it," I say and wink. I shake out the squeegee and stick it back in the bucket.

I reach for the pump. It's at $16.98. Fuck. I pull the pen out.

"Shit." I can't help saying it under my breath.

She looks back at the pump, then down at her hand, still clutching the wrinkled bills and change.

"I'm sorry," I say.

"I'm sure I can scrounge it up," she says.

"Don't worry about it. I should've been paying more attention. Flirting less."

She runs her hand through her hair, wets her lips, smiles.

"I'll take care of the difference," I say. "Maybe it will teach me a lesson."

"Thank you so much," she says, hanging halfway out the window now, her breasts rising out of her tube top like Hemingway's white hills. She sticks out a hand. "Daisy," she says. "You're like the best gas station attendant ever."

"A guy's got to be good at something."

She hands over the $11.85 and drives away, waving the whole time. Even as she merges into traffic.

COMMUNIST

"What kind of person reads?" Craig says, when he sees I've brought a book with me.

"Hopefully lots of people," I say and he makes a loud pffft sound.

"No one reads. Except magazines or the newspaper."

"All right then."

"Only squares read," he says. He even outlines a square with his fingers in the air. Like I might not get it.

"Guess I'm a square then," I say.

It's a slow afternoon. Craig smokes half a pack of cigarettes in less than an hour just for something to do. He alternates between menthols and full-flavored.

"Who does that?" I'd asked once.

"Your grandma," he said and blew a puff of smoke in my direction.

"What you reading?" he says, not looking at me, like he's asking how many clean shop rags we have left. "*The Communist Manifesto*?"

"Already read that," I say. His eyes dart at me.

"You are a little commie, aren't you?"

"You know it," I say. "A big flaming pinko."

A RV pulls in and behind it a blue Celica. "Dibs on the Celica," I say. RV's are always driven by an old man who wants to talk your ear off for the fifteen minutes it takes to fill the tank.

"Fucker," Craig says.

VACUUM GIRL

A tall, reedy brunette walks into the office. She holds out two dollar bills. "Can I get some quarters for the vacuum?" she asks. Her voice is soft. She's wearing a flowing brown dress past her knees. Her hair is wavy and untamed. Reminds me of Janis Joplin's but less fluffy.

I hand her eight quarters and she says, "Thanks" and lingers for a second before turning for the door.

She's got a small green pickup. A Ford Ranger. A canopy over the bed. The back end is pointed toward the side window of the office. She pulls down the tailgate. The bed is lined with shag carpet. She puts quarters in the vacuum and leans into the cab of the truck.

I go back to inventorying cigarettes, but can't help peeking out the window. Her legs stick out the door.

Cigarettes are not going to get counted this way. She finishes the cab. Puts more quarters in the machine and crawls into the back of the truck. She sits facing the office, vacuuming the shag carpet. I know I'm staring. Know she probably sees me.

She waves.

I wave back. Then she pulls her dress up to her waist. Even from the office, fifteen yards away at the most, I can see she's not wearing panties. She keeps vacuuming, a slanted grin on her face.

Cigarettes are not going to get counted.

The vacuum stops. She scoots out of the truck, brushes her dress off. She slams the tailgate shut and waves again before getting into the truck and driving away.

I turn back to the cigarettes, shaking my head. People wouldn't believe me if I told them the shit that happens working at a gas station.

I finish the inventory. It's starting to get dark out. It's six. Three more hours before I can close and head home.

"Excuse me."

I turn around. She's back.

"I'm parked behind the station," she says, and raises her

eyebrows. Like she's daring me. She walks out of the office and around the corner. I flip the closed sign and lock the door.

The tailgate is open and she's sitting in the back corner of the truck bed. I crawl in, pull the tailgate shut, close the lid of the canopy.

She lifts her dress over her head. She's completely naked underneath. Her small breasts glisten with sweat.

"It's a good thing I vacuumed today," she says and lays flat on the off-white carpet. "I know it sounds like a line, but I've never done this kind of thing before." She laughs nervously.

I can't quite say the same. "It's okay," I say. I flash a smile, "No need for a line, we're both here."

She raises her arms above her head until they touch the window of the cab. I kiss her nipples and she wraps her legs around me.

"You could get fired, huh?" she says and can't keep from smiling.

"We could get arrested," I say and lean down to kiss her pale stomach.

STARDOM

One of the suits is back. Craig is already off for the day, leaving me defenseless. I turn off the stereo before he gets to the office door.

"Hey," he says, and sticks out his hand. It's clear he doesn't remember my name.

"Craig's off," I say.

He nods. His name is Scott. He was probably in a frat. He's got a dark blue tie on and pleated gray slacks. His shoes probably cost more than I make in a pay period. He would probably refer to them as 'loafers.'

"We really want to make this station our focus," he says. "Really turn it around. We think it could do great business for us." He makes it sound like we're a fast food franchise. Another notch on a global corporation's belt. "Do you have any suggestions?"

Where to start? But he doesn't wait for me to say anything.

"We're thinking about adding oil change services."

Between the office and the car wash is a space that used to be leased to a local oil change service called Fast Change. They were forced to shut down after an old lady fell into the pit, cracking her skull. She died in the hospital three days later and her husband sued the owners of the company. They lost all three locations of the Fast Change. The bay has been deserted ever since.

It seems like it would cost a lot to open our own oil change service. More employees, more products, training. What happened to the car wash being the great cash cow?

I don't say any of that. I just nod. Say, "yeah" or "uh huh."

"All right," Scott says. "Just wanted to drop in on my way past." He shakes my hand again. "Thanks for your input."

"No problem," I say.

"We really think you're going to be a star for us," he says.

Okay. "Will there be heavy lifting?" I say, before I can stop myself.

He laughs. Points his finger at me like a gun. "Catch you later," he says.

SOUL

I don't know if I'd say I feel like my soul's been sucked out of me. But I'm dragging. And it's not just the drinking and not sleeping enough. It's not even the pills. It's definitely the job. I ask Craig if he finds pumping gas fulfilling.

"What do you take me for?" he says. "Do I look like some queer?"

"By the end of the day I feel pretty useless," I say. "What's the point? We get paid shit and do the same damn thing every day. And what's more whether we want to be or not, we're a part of an industry that is systematically destroying our economy and environment. We're the smallest, poorest cogs in a very evil machine."

Craig squirts Windex on the counter and wipes it dry. "It's a job," he says. "Jobs aren't supposed to be fulfilling. That's a stupid psychological term. You're an idealistic kid and I hate to ruin life for you, but there's no meaning. You work to pay bills. That's all."

Maybe it's what the guy meant when he said this job would steal my soul. Maybe it's not. Maybe I thought I'd be doing something else to support myself, even though I never had a clue what I wanted to do. Even if I had finished college. And probably the biggest maybe of all: maybe getting kicked out of school is finally catching up to me, months later.

"Working might just be the kick in the pants you need," my dad had said. But I wouldn't dare tell him he might have been right.

TYPES

I used to think I had a "type" of woman. That I had at least narrowed it down. But if anything I've found my definition expanding. Forty-year old women jogging by the station in spandex pants and jogging bras catch my attention as readily as the high school girls that walk past in jeans and T-shirts.

The last time I was with Sondra she laughingly asked me if she was the oldest woman I'd been with.

"Most experienced," I said, which got me an extra fifty bucks.

"I like flattery," she said. "Even if that's all it is."

When I left the next morning she said, "You're at the tail end of your sexual peak, I hope you're making full use of it."

"You know it," I said.

She never asks if I see other women, the answer is obvious enough. She just makes sure she always has a fresh pack of condoms when she calls me.

The whole thing is somewhere between a job and a normal sex life, I suppose. I enjoy the sex, but I don't feel any connection to Sondra or Catherine, or Catherine's friend Cynthia who has been calling me for a couple weeks now. I feel more connected to the gas station. The weirdest thing is not feeling weird about it. I get to have sex and I get paid. I've been able to save money for once, even if I don't know what I'm saving it for.

Cynthia was a psychology major before she popped out three kids with her banker husband. The first time we had sex she asked me how it felt.

"Don't worry," I said. "It was great."

She laughed. "I meant about having sex for money."

"Like I have money."

She thinks it's interesting that I don't have emotions tied to sex.

"I probably wouldn't be here if I did," I said. "How would I be able to justify having sex with married women?"

"That's what I meant," she said.

Then we went at it again.

I wondered if she was thinking about how it made me feel to keep from thinking about how it made her feel.

COLD

We get an early cold snap. Twenty degree lows. Craig's taking a couple vacation days and as "assistant manager" I have to cover his opening shift. At the station at 5:30, open at 6.

The heater's on the fritz. I go outside and hook up the hose, not realizing there's a hole in it. When I turn on the water a geyser shoots into the air and drenches me. First goddamn thing in the morning. Twenty degrees out, no heat, and soaked in cold water.

"You look a little wet," the first customer of the days says.

My dad would say, "Fucking duh." Instead I force a chuckle and say, "Little hose accident this morning."

Not that I've ever wanted to, but this is when I have the concrete realization that I never want to manage a gas station. "I should look for a better job," I say to myself.

I know that I won't. It's easier to stay with what I already have.

VICODIN

When P.J. gets to work for his swing shift he's wearing a neck brace. His eye sockets are sunken and bruised.

"What the hell happened?" I say, not even thinking about toning down my reaction for his sake.

A car ran him off the road on his way home. He was in the hospital all night.

"What are you doing here?" I ask.

He thinks he can make it through the shift with pain pills. "You want a couple?" he asks. "They gave me enough for a herd of elephants."

A couple Vicodin go a long way to making a day at work go by.

Every ring of the bell is a distant noise. Each customer a cloud.

My head is a balloon.

I send P.J. home, tell him I can handle the afternoon without help. He looks miserable.

"You should be laying down or something," I say.

He leaves me with a handful of Vicodin. I put them in the small outer pocket of my backpack. They'll come in handy.

I put on Led Zeppelin and sing along to "Dancing Days." There are no customers for the last two hours of work. I sing "Dancing Days" at least ten times. The delivery truck comes by and fills our tanks. We rarely need a delivery more than once a week. The truck driver eats a sandwich while the tanks fill. His hands are black with grease and grime. It stains the bread before it gets to his mouth. He doesn't notice.

I keep the stereo on, but I don't sing while he's there.

I wonder why I've never thought of taking pain pills at work. Take enough of anything and it's bound to make the day a bit more interesting. Right?

By the time I close the Vicodin has started wearing off, leaving me with a pounding headache. I head home to my futon and a half-empty bottle of whiskey.

NAMES

Running credit cards all day you see a lot of names. In my head I collect them. The various spellings, the foreign ones I can't pronounce, those of famous characters from TV shows or books, names shared with celebrities.

When Samuel Adams III fills with regular, I ask if there's any relation. He scowls at me. Says, "What do you think? "

I ask Gwen S. Prince, Esq. what the last part means. "Esquire," she says. I nod, washing the windshield of her Saab convertible "It's a fancy word for lawyer," she says.

Michael Fox doesn't look like he has a sense of humor, so I don't say a thing.

Gerald Ginsberg is a scrawny middle-aged man with reddish brown hair and freckles all over. He's not related to the poet or Supreme Court justice.

I misread a Topher as Gopher.

I decide if I ever have a kid I'll name him (or her) Pirate. How great would it be to have that name on your credit card? Or on letters? The possibilities are endless.

WHORING

I guess you could call it whoring. Could. I don't.

There are six women who have my number now. Six women who I allow to call me for sex. Who pay me for sex. Sondra created a monster. Not that I ever tell her that. Who could find the time, with business to attend to?

I'd be lying if I said I wasn't tired of it sometimes.

There are times where I am more than happy to slouch around my cruddy apartment letting the Beatles or Sex Pistols or Pixies act as my only company. But, I figure, entrepreneurs are all about striking while the iron's hot. Giving consumers what they demand. And I've been putting a lot of money away. I don't know what I'm saving it for yet, but my dad is always telling me, "time is money, only money can be saved. Unfortunately you never know when you'll need more of either."

So, I sleep with women. Housewives whose husbands pay more attention to their secretaries than their wives. Housewives who spend an hour a day in the gym, sweating themselves retarded to keep a glimpse of the figure they had in high school or college.

And I'm there for them. I give them what they need and want. In the end I'm getting sex on a daily basis and making more money than I do at my job. Making more money than many college graduates ever will. How's that for justice?

MORE CHANGES

It's Monday. My Saturday. My cell phone rings and shows work's number. "If you don't want to work on your day off," Craig said my first day on the job, "don't answer."

I don't.

The phone rings again. Shit.

I answer.

"You need to get to the station," Craig says. "Shit's going down."

I pull on some jeans and get in my car.

The suits are at the station. Craig and P.J. are, too. And another guy I don't recognize. He's dressed in jeans and a T-shirt, with a fleece vest to tie the ensemble together. He's got a mustache straight out of bad porn.

Turns out the company is opening an oil change service after all.

"This is Cal," one of the suits says, introducing Mr. Mustache. "He's going to co-manage with Craig."

Craig looks pissed.

"He's got a lot of experience in the oil changing business."

Cal shakes my hand.

"We're going to shut down for a couple days and he's going to train everybody."

Except P.J., that is. They're firing him. Cal's bringing in a couple people from the car wash he owns.

Craig's practically got steam coming out his ears. "Fuck this," he says to me when we have a moment alone. "I'm quitting." He smokes a cigarette, full flavor and calms himself down.

"If everyone wants to meet here at nine tomorrow," Cal says, "we can start getting everything ready."

So much for my weekend. On my way home I stop at the liquor store. Buy a half-gallon of vodka. I'm going to have a headache tomorrow anyway, I think, might as well enjoy the making of it.

TRAINING

Cal shows up with a box of doughnuts. "Figured we should start this the right way," he says.

He's wearing an outfit nearly identical to yesterday's. He's got a holster on his belt. The guy is wearing a handgun. I decide not ask about it just yet.

We have to take stock of what products have been left over from the Fast Change. It's a lot of counting boxes, checking product numbers. Cal promises us that tomorrow we'll learn how to service a car. I can't help laughing. I'm thankful he doesn't seem to notice.

We take a break for lunch and a teenage girl drives up.

"Hi, dad," she says.

Cal walks up to her and they hug. She's blonde. Her hair curls wildly, like a mane. She's short, probably not over five feet. Her perky rack is hugged by a gray T-shirt, probably from the GAP. She's dropped by to bring her daddy's lunch.

"This is my daughter, Olivia," Cal says.

She shakes my hand.

When we get back to work I'm on a ladder tossing boxes of oil filters down to Cal. Craig is off smoking. His third pack of the day.

"So," I say, "how old's your daughter?"

Cal glares up at me. "Don't even think about it," he says. "She's sixteen."

"No worries. Though, you should see if she wants to come by my apartment this weekend, I was thinking of having a party."

"There's a reason I carry a gun," Cal says.

I laugh. "I'm just giving you crap."

Within a week we are changing oil.

"You're a natural," Cal said to me.

I didn't know if I felt okay about taking that kind of compliment.

Within a week I've sneaked my number to Olivia who drops by to say hello to her dad almost every day. She's clearly a sheltered sixteen-year old. It's even clearer that it is my job to change that.

FiRST DAY

It's my first day as a lube technician. My schedule's changed. I work eight to four, Monday through Friday now. No more closing shifts, no more opening in Craig's place. I work the hours of the oil change bay and I'm only pumping gas when there's no oil to be changed.

I woke up late. I've felt rushed since the moment I opened my eyes. Didn't have time to put on any music while I showered. Didn't even have time for coffee.

I barely make it on time. I'm not used to having to be at work so early. There are already two cars lined up for oil changes. I head straight down the stairs of what we're now calling "Bay Two." My morning is started under a car.

I pull on the sliding tray that catches the draining oil and duck underneath it. When it's passed over my head I go to catch it with my left hand, but it's moving too fast. It hits the end of the track hard. Oil splashes out.

I watch it in slow motion. It is like a fountain.

Oil drenches my hair, face and uniform. It's even in my eyes. "Fuck."

I run back up the metal stairs, into the back room where the extra uniforms and other supplies are kept. I turn on the sink and stick my head underneath. Cal comes in.

"Everything all right?" he asks.

"Got a little soaked," I say.

He chuckles.

My eyes sting. I've gotten most of the oil off my face and arms.

Out of my hair. But there are no extra uniforms in my size.

The rest of the day is spent smelling like oil. Cal tells me to "watch the cussing in front of customers."

"That shit got me by surprise," I say and he nods.

He's taken to placing his handgun on top of the safe in the office. When there are no customers for oil changes Craig, Cal and me hang out in the office or by the pumps.

Cal parks his SUV in front of the station. It has a bumper sticker that says, "Handguns, A Man's Best Friend." There's also an NRA sticker in the window.

"You did great today," Cal says when I'm punching my time card.

I nod.

"You've picked it up fast."

I don't say that I'm a quick learner. I don't say it's not hard. I can tell he's being genuine.

"The smell of oil is practically coming out of my pores," I say.

"And that shit doesn't get you high. Just gives you a headache."

"Tomorrow you'll watch what you're doing," Cal says.

"Tomorrow I hopefully won't be in such a rush."

"You'll get the hang of it."

God, I hope not.

OLIVIA

Olivia calls.

I've gotten Friday off after going over forty hours in four days. The company doesn't like to pay overtime. Her dad is at work. Her lunch period just started and I tell her I'll pick her up.

"I have a car," she says.

I hadn't thought of that. We agree to meet at the Subway near the high school. I get there early and buy a large soda to pass the time. She's wearing a jean skirt and a yellow tank-top. She's holding a fleece jacket under her arm. What's with her family and fleece? She waves at her friends and comes to my table

"So, what do you want to do?"

"I don't know," she says. "Whatever you want."

"I'll have you back when school lets out."

She looks at me sheepishly.

"I've never cut before," she says.

"There's a first time for everything," I say and take her hand, leading her to my car.

"Do you want me to follow you?"

I shake my head. "I'll bring you back."

We go to my apartment and I put a frozen pizza in the oven. Open a bottle of cheap wine.

"I've had alcohol before," she had said in the car, trying to prove she wasn't completely sheltered. "Beer, and wine coolers." She takes a sip of the wine and her facial muscles tighten, trying not to show the distaste.

"It takes some getting used to," I say. "Like anything good, you've got to work for it."

I sit next to her on the futon, which thankfully I'd taken my blanket off of when I woke up.

She lays her head against my shoulder, leans it back. We kiss.

"I want you to be my first," she says.

I finish my glass of wine. Her virginity isn't a surprise, my reaction is. "I could go to jail," I say.

"No one will ever know."

"Your dad would kill me before I even got to jail."

She laughs.

"You're only sixteen," I say.

"Most of the girls I know have had sex, it's not a big deal."

"Trust me, I'd love to fuck you."

She kisses me. Buries her hand in my pants. "Then do it," she says.

I drop her off at the Subway parking lot thirty minutes after school has gotten out.

"My dad's still at work," she said. "He won't know I wasn't home on time."

That's when we went for a second time.

"I'm just getting the hang of it," she said when we were getting dressed. "We should do it again."

I laughed and chugged a glass of water. "You'll be the death of me with that attitude."

Before she gets out of my car she leans over and kisses me.

"I think your cum is leaking down my leg," she says, quietly into my ear, like someone else might be hiding in my car.

"Sorry," I say and she kisses me again.

"No biggie." Then she's out of the car and closing the door. "Talk to you soon," she says.

I watch her get into her car and drive away. When she gets home I know she'll shower and change her clothes. And I wonder if she's a good enough liar to keep anyone from finding out.

CHANGING OIL

I spend most of my time at work underneath cars. In less than a month I know what side of the engine the oil filter will be on by the make of the car. My arms are black with grease from reaching into the innards of cars, changing filters and fluids. Shop rags don't clean that shit, they just make it gray. Until your skin becomes colorless, ashen.

I breathe exhaust.

I begin to long for moments standing outside of the office just for fresh air. The regular customers I'd gotten used to, the lesbian whose butch girlfriend glared at me, the guy with his dirty jokes, the college campus' mailman, the housewives, they don't exist anymore. When I stumble into one of them at the pumps they ask where I've been.

"I'm changing oil now."

CODE TWELVE

We have codes so customers won't know if something's gone wrong during their oil change. Code five means you've got a leak. Code two means "if you don't get down here fast something bad is going to happen." There is a handful of them. I don't remember them too well, except code twelve. Code twelve is when there's a hot girl in the vicinity. No shit.

Cal says it started in the chain he used to work for, that his brothers own. "Go into any of them and yell 'code twelve' and you'll see a dozen heads pop out of every direction like little prairie dogs."

Cal yells it. "Code twelve." Like it's a fire drill.

It's Office Girl.

"Haven't seen you around much," she says to me, while Craig hands her cigarettes.

"They've stuck me under the cars," I say, and she laughs like it's a joke.

"See you around," she says, turning and strutting out of the office and back across the street. The slit in her black skirt is longer than it used to be, I think. Her thighs are as tan as her arms.

"Whooee," Cal says. "I think she likes you."

"Everybody likes me," I say. "I'm a goddamn joy."

THE BOMB

Olivia calls me every night. She talks about things like what some girl said in economics class. I keep the TV volume on low and try to make out what's being said in stupid shows.

The fourth time she comes over it's a Saturday. She told her dad she's going to the mall. We do it twice, taking a break in between to eat. She drinks three beers.

"I think I'm in love with you," she says and I tell her she's drunk.

"We should get married."

She's really drunk.

"I'm pregnant," she says and throws up on my kitchen floor. I walk her to the bathroom and help her clean her face and hair. I clean the floor.

"You're pregnant?"

She nods. "I took a test."

I crack another beer and drain it.

"Don't worry," she says. "I'm going to get rid of it. My father can't find out or he'd kill me."

I stare at the wall.

"I just thought you should know."

"Are you sure?"

"I'm sixteen, there's no way I'm having a baby yet." She grabs her sweatshirt and tugs it over her head. "I better go," she says. "Don't want anyone getting suspicious."

She leans down and kisses me. I try to kiss back, telling myself nothing's different.

THE RECORD

I go to work hung-over.

"You look dead," Craig says.

"You tie one on last night?" Cal asks.

"Yeah," I say for lack of a better response.

"Nice," he says. "Enjoy it while you're young."

I do seventeen oil changes. Our store record. "We should celebrate or something," Cal says, as we're punching out our time cards.

So we go to a bar a couple blocks from the station. He buys me a Jack and Coke.

"You're a damn good worker," he says. "But you're also a lot smarter than most people who do this kind of work."

I want to puke.

"Don't get me wrong, there's no one I'd rather have working for me, but why aren't you out looking for a better job?"

"Craig was the only person who would hire me when I started applying for jobs after I got kicked out of school."

"You're sticking it out because of loyalty?"

"And laziness," I say. "I was doing some other work on the side, that made me really good money, but I've stopped answering the phone when they call."

Cal nods like he knows what I'm talking about. People do that a lot.

"Well," he says between ordering us another round, "I won't lecture you, but I've got one piece of advice: don't get stuck doing something you don't want to be doing. Time moves a lot faster than you think and soon you'll be my age and there really won't be a reason to quit and do something else."

We finish our second round and order a third.

"My treat," I say.

Cal pats me on the back. "You know most people wouldn't believe me, but I love changing oil. I don't know why, but I always have."

RETURN

It's been over two weeks since I've heard from Olivia, but when I get home from work she's waiting at my front door.

"Everything all right?" I ask.

"Of course," she says and kisses me with a big smile plastered on her face.

"I haven't heard from you in a while."

"I just needed some time to get it out of my system," she says.

I guess she wasn't going for a pun. I unlock the front door and we go inside. She's on me instantly. Kissing, tugging at my belt, shrugging out of her jeans.

This is so dysfunctional, I think, picking her up and laying her on the couch. Pulling her orange panties down her legs. She bites my lip, pulls me into her. She is sweating more than me by the time we're done.

"Do you have any beer?" she asks, and I tell her I'm out.

"Just whiskey," I say and she shrugs.

She gets up and walks to the kitchen, her pale pink body glowing in the dim light of the apartment—I hadn't even turned on the lights when we came in.

She drinks straight from the bottle. Passes it to me.

"I'm sorry," she says.

I tell her there's nothing to apologize for. If anything it should be me saying sorry, but I don't.

"I guess this is the real world," she says, like she's playing the role of grown-up. "I like fucking you," she says and I realize I'd never heard her cuss before. "It makes everything fall away, like it's just us alone in the universe."

I don't see the comfort in that, but she straddles me and pushes on my shoulders to lay me down.

"Aren't your parents going to wonder where you are?" It's ten o'clock, and I remember Olivia saying her curfew on weeknights is ten.

She shrugs, her new favorite form of body language. She takes another drink from the bottle. "Can't I stay with you tonight? I'll call them and say I have to finish a project with a friend and it'd be easier to just crash at her house."

In the morning when I head to work she's still sleeping, bits of naked flesh peeking out from the tangled blanket. I wonder if she'll still be there when I get home. But she's not. There's just a note taped to the refrigerator. "Sorry I'm such a mess. Thanks for letting me stay with you. I'll call you soon. Love, Olivia."

BUSHED

Cal's no help. I've got three cars in line for oil changes and he's off on his cell phone. I run clipboards out to each car, getting the make and model of their cars so I can enter it in our computer system and see what parts they take. I run under the cars and drain the oil, run back upstairs and check the fluid levels. Run downstairs and change the oil filter, back upstairs to check the tire pressure.

It's one o'clock and I'm bushed.

I run my blackened hand through my hair, leaving streaks of grease. I don't care anymore. I have to clean my shower every other day it gets so dirty.

Cal snaps his phone shut. "Olivia's been acting crazy," he says.

My throat goes dry.

"We lost our oldest daughter to meth, but I didn't think Olivia would follow her lead."

"She's doing meth?"

"We don't know. She's been acting different lately, but we don't know what's going on." Cal tucks his phone into the case he carries on his belt next to the holster. "Maybe it wouldn't have been such a bad thing to have her interested in a guy like you," he says. "At least you work hard and stick to alcohol for your vices."

"She's a teenager," I say. "I'm not that far removed and teenage girls act insane sometimes, but that doesn't mean she's on drugs."

"I hope you're right," he says, drumming his hands on the office counter.

NO CHARGE

I top off fluids and fill tires. "How much?" people ask, the fright instilled by the ever-rising gas prices carrying over to my new position at the station.

"No charge," I say. Sadly this impresses people.

On the other hand when I tell them it'll be $39.95 for an oil change, they look at me like I'm evil. Like I'm the suit in the office, or the board of directors from a big oil company. Like I sleep under a blanket of hundred dollar bills when I go home at night. I have money in the bank, but it's sure as hell not from this piece of shit job, I want to yell at them. Instead I say, "Your air filter's shot" and when they ask how much a new one costs I tell them $24.99.

You get enough of those looks from people and some days you can't help thinking you're the devil.

Some days maybe it's true.

I sell them new air filters, full radiator flushes, windshield wipers, brake fluid. And when I'm done I tell them about our fabulous state-of-the-art car wash, with it's triple-wax deluxe wash.

For all I know, I'm the anti-Christ.

NEW

My phone rings. It's Olivia. The women from before, the women who gave me a second job, one any man would kill for, have stopped calling after weeks of me not answering.

"Your dad's been worried about you," I say and she says he has no reason to. "He thinks your doing meth."

She giggles. "I'm not doing meth," she says.

"Promise?"

She tells me stop acting like her parents. "A guy at school asked me out today," she says and inhales loudly, as if expecting me to reach through the phone and smack her.

"That's great," I say and mean it.

"You're not jealous? Don't you want me for yourself ? I told him I had to think about it."

"It wouldn't have worked between us," I say. "And you know that. There's been plenty of proof. It'd be good for you to date someone your age."

"Fuck," she says. "You know I meant it when I told you I loved you."

"I know."

"Fuck."

"I hope he treats you well," I say. "Better than I did. You deserve that at least."

"Can I come over?"

It's a question I don't want to answer. If she comes over I know we'll have sex, tangling ourselves even further. Part of me wants that. Wants her fresh, naked body lying underneath me. The other part of me wants to let her have her life back, whether she sees it that way or not.

"We'd just end up fucking," I say.

"I know," she says, which makes it harder to refuse.

"I don't want to feel like I've ruined your life anymore than I already have."

"Fuck," she says and it still sounds new coming out of her mouth.

SICK DAY

I'm near-puking drunk when I show up to work.

"Jesus," Craig says. "I'll tell Cal you're sick. You need to get home."

"And walk your happy ass there," he says when I head for my car. "What the hell's wrong with you?"

I stop at the liquor store on my way home. Stock up on half-gallons of vodka, rum, and whiskey. The guy running the store adds a brochure on alcoholism to my bag.

"There's a meeting tonight at the Episcopal church," he says. "You might think about dropping in."

I thank him with my middle finger.

At home I turn on the TV to some stupid daytime talk show and blast the stereo at the same time. No time like the present for some Johnny Cash. The only thing I will give my dad credit for, teaching me about *the man in black*.

I sing along until I run out of breath, stumbling between the kitchen and couch. I finish the last half of a pint glass full of whiskey in one long drink.

LANDSCAPING

Craig shows up at my door.

"I'm quitting," he says. "And you need to get your shit together or they'll fire you."

He lists the ways I've been fucking up. Showing up drunk or hung-over. Puking behind the station. Once. (I thought I'd washed it away with the hose before anyone had noticed). Calling in sick. Showing up late. Not screwing an oil filter on all the way. Breaking a car's windshield wiper while trying to install a new blade.

"I don't know how Cal hasn't noticed," he says.

He could go on for hours. He says things like "I don't know what happened to you" and "I thought you were better than this."

"Anyway," he says. "I told them I'm done and I thought you should know."

"What are you going to do?"

"Landscaping," he says. "I figure it's better than pumping gas."

A week later I see him at a 76 station, wearing their cherry red uniform and washing someone's back windshield while the gas tank fills.

COCAINE BLUES

I chop three white lines out on the kitchen counter. Suck them up one by one.

I scrounge in my backpack. Find the Vicodin P.J. gave me the day I let him go home. I take three.

I put on *Come On Pilgrim* and sing "Caribou" over and over. My life has grown repetitive, only the soundtrack changing.

I sit on the floor of the shower and let the warm water pelt my face. I wake up and the water is like ice. Goosebumps blanket my skin. I'm shivering. My head pounds.

I walk naked and dripping wet to the kitchen. I drink vodka. Maybe rum. I think I mixed the two at some point.

I run back to the bathroom and stick my head in the toilet. I vomit until my throat feels like it's clawing its way out of my neck.

I wrap myself in a blanket and fall asleep in the hallway.

IDIOTS AND ASSHOLES

The guys Cal has brought in from his car wash are idiots and assholes. Their names are Mitch and Barry. Barry's not so bad on his own, but around Mitch he acts like a douche clone. Mitch thinks he's better than me because he's two years older and wears it like it makes him one step below God.

Mitch brings a portable TV with him to work and when there are no customers for oil changes he sits on a stool watching Jerry Springer. He thinks he's too good to pump gas, as if changing oil is above all that. "I'm a lube technician," he says, like it's not just some bullshit term someone made up to sound like they knew what they were doing.

"We're all lube technicians," I say and he scoffs.

"Cal told me I'm here to change oil," he says.

"You're here to work, you fucking ape."

A car pulls up and I go to fill the tank.

"You should watch who you call names," he says when the car has pulled away.

I'm not mad at him. I'm mad at people who think they are better than me. I'm mad at people who don't think they have to work to make it through life.

"Where'd you learn to be such a douche?" I say and that gets Mitch off his stool.

He stands right in front of me, his nose an inch or two from mine. In this situation Craig would be bugging his eyes out and saying, "I've seen some shit, man, you don't want to mess with me." I knee Mitch in the groin and when he's doubled over I punch him in the top of the head with every ounce of strength I have left. He hits the floor with a noise like a balloon deflating.

When he gets to his feet again, Mitch brushes himself off and says, "You're so fired."

I laugh.

"What are you laughing about?" He touches the side of his hand to his mouth, checking for blood. There is none.

I laugh again. "If they fire me that leaves you to pump the gas, idiot. Then how are you going to sit on your ass?"

He flips me off and walks out of the office and around the corner to the bathroom. When he comes out a car is pulling up, all it takes is one look and he's at the driver's window. "What can I do for you?"

SAVED BY AN OIL CHANGE

I'm back to my old schedule I change oil until five and then I stick around and finish off the night pumping gas. It's like having two shitty jobs in one. The only good thing is that Mitch has been moved to working weekends. The rest of the week he stays at Cal's car wash.

Cal says Olivia is picking him up lunch and asks if I want anything. I shake my head. I haven't seen her in weeks. Every once and a while Cal says something like, "Thank God things have stabilized with Olivia," or "Guess it was nothing after all." These things are usually followed by sentiments about how I don't look like I'm eating enough lately.

"You're looking rough," he says. But he always laughs it off. "Having too much fun being young," he says. I cough out chuckles and he slaps me on the back.

Olivia drives up a little after noon. She looks like the first day I met her. Maybe her tits have gotten a little bigger. Or she's wearing a push-up bra.

She says, "Hi" and "How are you boys doing?"

"Hi, sweetie," Cal says and kisses her forehead when she hands him a bag of fast food.

Part of me wants a moment alone with her. Or for her to slip me a note. Part of me is angry. This is the impact I had on you, I think. It's like nothing ever happened. Part of me wants to slap her.

I'm saved by a car pulling in for an oil change. "The works," the driver says, peeling off his sunglasses. This will keep me busy for an hour, I think and direct him into the bay, so his Malibu is parked over the pit. Then I head down the stairs.

MOM

It's my mom's birthday. I call her and she asks if I'm coming to dinner at her house. My brother's cooking. I tell her I can't.

"Is everything all right?" she asks, and I know her patented three question grilling is coming. "Are you on drugs? Are you drinking? Did you get someone pregnant?" She asks the same three questions every time I call. It's why I stopped calling except on her birthday and Mother's Day.

There was a time I could answer all three with firm no's.

Now I say, "Mom, give it a rest" and she goes silent.

"You know," she says. "We only live ten minutes from you and we never see you."

"I work a lot."

"I thought when you moved back home from school it was to be closer to family."

"I don't know why I moved back, mom. I got kicked out and I didn't know what else to do."

She makes a 'hmm' sound in a 50's sitcom mom sort of way.

"I just wanted to call and wish you a happy birthday," I say. I know on the other end of the line she's nodding, responding to me in a way she still doesn't realize can't be translated over the phone.

"I love you," she says.

"You too," I say and hang up.

GETTING RIGHT

"I need someone I can rely on," Cal says. "I don't know what's been going on, but I know you're a good worker if you can move past whatever it is."

I know by the way he's phrasing everything that the suits have told him to fire me. That he's convinced them to give me a chance to turn it around.

"You're right," I say. "I've been fucking up. But I can pull it together."

He gives me three extra days off and tells me to come back Monday with my head on straight. He shakes my hand. Like we're just meeting or saying goodbye.

Maybe both.

BEARDED

I stopped shaving a couple weeks ago and now I've got a decent blonde beard covering my face. Cal says it makes me look like a down and out thirty-five year old.

"That's what I'm going for," I say.

He tells me I should go out and find a woman. Out of boredom I go to a bar after work. I don't change, just take off my uniform shirt.

I order a White Russian because I'm craving something thick. There's a scrawny brunette sitting by herself. Part of me wants to say something, but I don't.

"Stood up," the brunette says, standing up and moving to the stool next to me. "Mind if I pretend I was on this stool all along?"

"Sure thing," I say. "What kind of idiot would stand you up?" Her name is Sarah and she tells me about the guy she met last night at another bar when she was out with her friends from school.

"Third year English major," she says. "Anyway he told me he'd meet me here tonight. Guess I fell for it."

"I won't tell anyone," I say.

We have a couple drinks and she tells me that she loves Victorian poetry. That she is a hobbyist photographer. "Mostly self-portraits."

"My dad is a photographer," I say and she lights up.

She's practically glowing with enthusiasm. "This is probably stupid," she says. "But do you want to come to my apartment?"

"Sure."

She shares an apartment with another girl, so we're quiet going in. She closes her bedroom door with two hands. She sits on the floor with her back against the side of her bed. I sit across from her, not knowing what else to do.

"Can I take your picture?"

I say okay, and she kneels at my side, taking a profile shot.

"Do you want to take mine?"

I hold the camera, an am reminded of my childhood, my

dad teaching me how to "point and shoot." The more complicated things, he told me, could wait until I was older. He wasn't kidding.

Sarah peels her clothes off. She sits back in front of her bed and tucks her legs up against her chest. I point the camera and look at her naked body, all skin and protruding bones in the viewfinder.

For all her talk of Victorian poetry and other clichéd nonsense I realize she's not all that girly. She has bruises on her legs and dirt under her fingernails. She doesn't wear lipstick. She kisses in sporadic bursts, lunging at my lips, darting her tongue in and out of my mouth.

When we fuck she grunts and screams. Says she'll have to apologize to her roommate in the morning. When we're done she says I'm the only guy who has given her an orgasm.

"I've only done that with a vibrator," she says.

I laugh. "Beginner's luck," I say.

"Yeah right," she says.

She tells me she's going to write a poem about our sex and I ignore the cheesiness of such a claim. She asks me to take another picture of her.

"Post-Passion," she says.

While I'm focusing her camera lens she says, "Have you ever wondered what it would be like to be a prostitute?" For a second I think about telling her I don't need to wonder. It would probably make her year. The best story she'd have to tell from her college years. Instead I shake my head and snap the picture.

She runs her fingers in my beard and asks if we're having a one-night stand.

"It can be whatever you want it to be," I say.

FAME

I'm filling the tank of a Subaru and a little girl sticks her head out of the back window. She takes a deep breath and her dad turns and asks what she's doing.

"I like the smell of gas," she says and the dad tells her to sit back in her seat.

"Don't be silly," he says and notices me laughing. "See," he says. "Even the man thinks you're being silly."

I shake my head. "Actually I like the smell of gas, too." The little girl grins and the dad rolls his eyes.

I bring his credit card receipt for him to sign. "If I can get your autograph," I say, another routine.

The little girl snorts. "He's not famous," she says.

I raise my eyebrows. "You never know," I say. "He could be one day."

"Really?" she says.

I nod. Her eyes grow wide. "You could be famous one day dad," she says as he rolls up his window and drives away.

SKATERS

Skateboarders are jumping the steps behind the station. I walk around the corner of the building and stand there with my arms folded.

"What's up?" one of them says, nodding his head at me.

"You guys can't skate here," I say.

"Come on," says another. "Do you really want to be *the man*, shoving stupid rules down peoples' throats?"

"In this case, yes I do."

They are shocked at first, but the first one to talk recovers and asks why they can't skate on the steps.

"First because it's private property," I say. "Secondly because the noise bothers me. And thirdly because I feel like telling you to scram."

They flip me off. Call me an asshole and other names. I wave as they skate down the street.

FUNNY

All my "dates" with Sarah end the same. She gets naked and curls up. Asks me to take pictures.

"You take the best ones," she says.

Then we go at it. Sometimes three or four times before she gets tired and I go home.

She says she read a poem about our sex in front her writing class. One day, she says, she'll let me read it. I nod and hope she won't. She thinks there's a secret to how I make her come every time we do it. I tell her there isn't.

"Just a freak thing," I say.

Spring break is coming up and she says she wishes I could come back to Colorado with her and meet her parents. I tell her that's a ways off. She pouts until I grab her camera, then she poses.

"You should be a photographer," she says. "Like your dad."

I say, "You should be a comedian," which she doesn't find funny.

FLASHBACK

I recognize the car as soon as Sondra pulls into the station.

"I thought you were dead," she says. I shake my head and start filling her tank. "I thought I was going to have find a new boy toy."

"You do," I say and she raises an eyebrow. "I've got a girlfriend."

She asks if it's serious and I freeze.

"It's sex without money changing hands," I say, instantly regretting it.

"Don't we get one last time?" she asks and I start washing her windshield. "Look if it has to be done we might as well go all out." I press the squeegee harder against the glass. "I have two thousand dollars in my purse. It's yours for one more night."

The pump clicks off.

"Or do you have plans with your girlfriend tonight?"

"She's home for spring break," I say.

I agree to go to her house after work.

"It'll be like old times," she says. "Though I'm not sure about the beard."

"You don't have to be," I say and she blows me a kiss as she drives off.

It's like a flashback. Like walking into a museum. Then again her house always had that feel. She's in a green skirt and white blouse.

"The shower's running for you," she says and I head up the stairs, knowing she'll be waiting for me with a drink when I get out.

She's laying on her side on the bed as I dry off and wrap the towel around my waist.

"Was I responsible for your sexual awakening?" she asks.

I tell her I don't know what that means.

"Tell me about how you lost your virginity." I sit next to her on the bed and she runs her hand under the towel, up my thigh.

"It was my brother's secretary," I say. "She and her husband worked opposite shifts and I saw her walking home in the rain, so I pulled over and asked if she wanted a ride home."

"She did," Sondra says.

"She thanked me and I told her to thank my mom for raising me right."

Sondra chuckles, continues rubbing my thigh slowly.

"In the parking lot outside her apartment she slipped off her panties and pushed up her skirt. Straddled me in the driver's seat."

"While her husband was sleeping inside?"

"And her two-year old son."

"Do you feel guilty?"

"When did you become a therapist?" I say and she pulls her hand out from under the towel.

"Sorry," she says. "Just curious."

She finishes off a full glass of wine and looks back at me. "We don't have to have sex," she says. "I'll still give you the money just because I like you."

"For two thousand dollars you deserve the best fuck I can give you," I say and her face lights up, takes ten years off her age.

"Can I make one more request?" she asks and I tell her she's entitled. "Can I videotape you ravaging me?"

"You've got a kinky streak, don't you?"

Her cheeks begin to blush, something I didn't think possible

"If it's going to be the last time," she says. "It would be nice to have a souvenir."

"It's a bit over the top for me," I say. "But I guess I'll make an exception."

She kisses my cheek and practically hops off the bed. "I'll be right back," she says.

I was supposed to call Sarah an hour ago, but I didn't. I'll call tomorrow. Tell her I was exhausted after work. That I crashed as soon as I got home. Sondra comes back in the room with a video camera and a tripod.

"My husband uses it for work," she says. "Depositions."

I wear myself out. I put everything I have into it. I try to tell myself it's an act of charity. That I'm doing it for Sondra's sake.

But I'm doing it for me. Thrusting so hard that Sondra is holding onto the headboard with both hands. She comes twice, but I don't stop. I am possessed. I slam into her harder and harder, until I finish and go limp. My body slumps next to hers on the bed.

"You were a mad man," she says.

All I can do is pant like a dog on a hundred degree day. "Worth it?" I ask between breaths.

"I may not need sex again for the rest of my life," she says. She gets up, turns off the camera and goes into the bathroom, closing the door behind her.

BOB DYLAN

Blonde On Blonde has become my work album. When we close the oil change down for the day and I'm the only one left at the station I put it in the stereo and listen to it on repeat until I close up and head home.

"Bob Dylan," customers say and I nod. This astute observation is usually followed by, "Right on." People are articulate.

An old guy looking for a pack of Virginia Slims tells me about seeing Dylan perform at the Newport Folk Festival in 1965. I try not to look in awe. Tell him about seeing Dylan in Eugene. "He mostly played keyboard all night," I say. "It was weird. But he did pick up a guitar to cover 'Brown Sugar.'"

I sell the old man our last three packs of Virginia Slims. I don't tell him they've been on the shelf for longer than I've worked here. That they'll probably smoke like kindling.

I wonder if he'll think I cheated him.

These kind of questions have been popping into my head lately. If people think I'm responsible for rising gas prices because I work at a gas station what else do they think I'm to blame for? Our continuous wars for the sake of oil? Arsonists who use gasoline to start fires? The possibilities are endless. And, as ridiculous as they might be, they haunt me.

When I need a distraction I sing, "Just Like A Woman" dragging out syllables like Dylan does. I don't know why this makes me feel better.

VOICEMAILS

Craig calls me in the middle of the night and leaves drunken messages on my voicemail.

"Hey, Cuntface," he says. "Fuck you. Fuck you Cuntface." He laughs like a maniac and hangs up.

Sometimes he slurs so bad I can barely make it out.

"WhasstupButtlickhahafuckerdumbfuggedstopyousuck-gormanassholefuck."

Sometimes he almost pulls it off.

"Hey, it's Craig. What are you up to? Want to get a beer?" Then he laughs and it deteriorates. "Huh, Assface? You there? Let's get a beer, Dumbfuck."

MOHAWK

It was a long day of oil changes. My skin is more grease than flesh-colored. I stay in the shower until the hot water becomes cold and my hands are wrinkled like raisins. I stand in front of the mirror, decide to give myself a mohawk.

I pull out the clippers I bought when I started growing my beard and plug them in. Running them over my scalp, I watch the hair fall to the bathroom floor. It doesn't take long and I am left with a blonde mohawk about two and a half inches long.

My reflection makes me laugh. Standing there naked with hair trimmings stuck to my shoulders, chest, and stomach. "Vroom vroom," I say holding the clippers in the air.

Later I start to wonder what people will think. Cal. Sarah. What Sondra would think. Or Olivia. Craig, my father, Carey and other friends from school who stopped calling after the first month of me being kicked out and moving home. I should take a picture, I think. But I don't have a camera. It will have to wait until Sarah is back from Colorado.

THE MYSTERY

I'd forgotten I gave Sarah a key to my apartment. When I get home from work she's laying naked in the center of the futon couch, which she's pulled out into a bed.

"Miss me?" she asks and I say yes, because that's how you answer that question.

She pulls me on top of her.

"I need to shower," I say.

"I'll join you," she says.

Between soaping my body she kisses nearly every inch of my skin.

"Longest two weeks ever," she says.

I nod. She says she can live with the mohawk. That she might even grow to like it.

"What possessed you?" she asks.

"I don't know," I say. "Just got the urge."

"You seem different," she says.

I tell her it was just a long day. "Pumping gas is amazingly exhausting."

She nods, even though she's never had a job. I know at this moment that we will break up. When is the only mystery left.

"I love you," she says, then covers her mouth like she just swore at me. "Sorry," she says. "I've been wanting to say that to you."

Why, is what I want to say. Why in God's name would you love me, or even think you do? Instead I say, "Don't worry about it. I love you, too."

I've never said it before and here I am saying it to someone not because I actually feel that way, but because I don't want to have a fight. Because I don't want to yell or be yelled at. Because she is naked and goosebumps are forming around her hard nipples, and I want to fall asleep with them pressed against my face.

We don't bother drying off. We fall against the bathroom wall, the towel rack lodged between my shoulder blades. She bites my bottom lip. Grinds her bony body into mine. She bites my shoulder, my chest, my neck. I push the door open and we tumble toward the futon. She looks at me like a wild animal.

"Two weeks is too long," she says and reaches to guide me inside her.

She fucks me like it's been years. And I realize this is how Sondra must have felt. Having someone use you to take out all the repression in their head. Like bouncing wildly on top of me will free a part of her she still doesn't understand. This goes on all night and I'm thankful I don't have to work. We take breaks for water, or to pee, but then she jumps on me, pins me back and disappears until one of us has an orgasm.

"I'm exhausted," I say and she laughs.

"It's good to be home," she says. "I love you," she says, curling up against me with her head on my chest.

I don't say anything at all.

TEAMWORK

Cal's been talking to the suits. "They're thinking of starting a chain of Quick Stops," he said, referring to the name they'd finally settled on for the oil change bay.

Quick Stop. It wasn't exactly genius.

"I told them they should hire us to run them," he says, and I practically snort. "We're a good team."

He's sincere, and even though he's old enough to be my dad, it's this singular quality that makes me feel like I'm in a parental position, rather than him.

"That's not going to happen," I say.

He asks why not.

"They said they were going to turn this station around and that hasn't happened yet. I have trouble believing their commitment."

"They're serious," he says.

"They're ADD," I say. "They have an idea of how to improve their business, they go gung ho for it until someone else comes up with an idea, then you get left midway with the last project."

"You could be making a lot more money," he says. "Maybe start working on salary."

"If it happens, all right," I say. "But I don't believe in getting my hopes up."

NIGHTMARE

I dream I am walking through the layers of hell. All the damned residents look at me with disgust. It's not as hot as I'd expect and everything is a pale blue color, like ice.

I keep asking myself "What am I doing here?" Though the whole thing makes perfect sense. The bigger question is why am I acting like an idiot and pretending I don't belong.

I tell myself there will be plenty of people I know, but I don't see any of them.

It's not until I wake up and splash water on my face that I realize I was the devil in the dream. That it wasn't disgust people were looking at me with, but hatred. That I wasn't on an idle stroll, but surveying my territory.

It's such an obvious dream. So full of potential for the dream interpreting therapists and psychology students.

It was just a dream.

I drink two shots of rum and fall back asleep.

THE HUSBAND

A Jaguar pulls into the station. One of the pre-Ford buyout Jags. A tall lean man with white hair steps out. He walks into the office and stands at the counter staring at me.

"Do you know who I am?" he asks.

I say no, because I don't.

"I'm Alex Muth," he says and I still don't know. "My wife's the woman you've been sleeping with."

I nearly ask him to clarify. By the car and his age he has to be Sondra's husband.

"Who the hell do you think you are?" he says.

Cal comes around the corner from closing the bay doors to the Quick Stop. Cal looks at me, gives me a look like "Is everything all right?"

I shrug.

"Can I help you, sir?" Cal asks, and Sondra's husband turns.

"This little shit's been sleeping with my wife."

"I'm sorry to hear that," Cal says. "But I don't think this is the appropriate way to handle the situation."

"You're right." Sondra's husband turns back to look at me. "I'm going to sue you for everything you've got."

I can't help myself. "Are you kidding? I pump gas for a living. I don't have anything. I barely make enough money to pay my bills."

It's obvious he hadn't thought of that.

"Just stay the hell away from my wife." He takes a tape from his pocket and throws it at me. "You can keep your smutty video you pervert."

I want to tell him he should be having this talk with his wife, but I don't. He gets in his car, revs the engine, and drives away.

"What was that about?" Cal asks, pulling his handgun from on top of the safe and replacing it in his holster.

"I was sleeping with his wife," I say.

He laughs. "And videotaping it?"

"That was her idea. She paid me a lot of money to do that."

"Holy shit, you're a little man-whore," Cal says, laughing so hard his eyes are tearing up. "I can't say I'd ever have seen it coming." He slaps me on the back. "Shit," he says. "I couldn't be prouder if you were my own son."

OVER

Like most nights Sarah is already at my apartment when I get home. I walk in and she doesn't even look up from the TV. It takes a second for me to realize what she's watching, but I don't believe it. I smashed the tape Sondra's husband threw at me.

Sarah turns and her face is covered in running mascara. "Guess what I got in the mail," she says, her voice reduced to small squeaks. "What is this?"

How do you explain something like that, I wonder. There's no point lying. Saying it was from before we got together. If for no other reason than that the date is in the lower right corner of the video.

"There's no way to make it sound okay," I say.

"You're fucking-a-right there isn't," Sarah says, suddenly yelling. She throws a pillow at me. "She's old," she says. "Wasn't I good enough for you?"

I nod.

"Aren't you going to say anything?"

"The truth isn't very attractive."

"What? Have you been sleeping around the whole time we were together?"

"No, just that once."

The tape is still playing. Out of the corner of my eye I see the flashes of frantic movement.

"Tell me there's an explanation," Sarah says. "Tell me something."

"Okay," I say.

I walk to the kitchen and pour two glasses of whiskey. I give one to Sarah and sit on the floor across from her, where I can't see the TV.

"Before we got together I slept with women for money."

"Oh, my god," she says. "That's disgusting."

"I stopped when I started seeing another girl. She got pregnant and had an abortion. We broke up." I'm looking for the simplest way to tell the story. "I didn't take the whole thing very well, but then we met."

"Don't try to sound sweet," she says and I apologize.

"You were gone for spring break, and this woman," I say pointing at the TV. "Came into the station wondering why I'd stopped answering her calls. I told her I was seeing someone. She asked if we could have one more night together and I said no. Then she offered me two thousand dollars. That's more than two months of pumping gas."

"There's something wrong with you. You're sick."

She's probably right.

"Look, I'm sorry. I feel bad about it, but I don't expect you to believe me or forgive me."

"Fuck you," she says. "Don't pretend to be a good person."

I don't move from my place on the floor while she stomps out the door and slams it behind her. To think, she wanted to introduce me to her family. She calls in the middle of the night and sobs for thirty minutes. Says, "why" over and over. I say nothing.

"I hate myself for wishing I was sleeping with you right now," she says.

"Don't worry," I say. "You don't ever have to see me again."

"You don't get it at all," she says and hangs up.

BAD DAY

A brown Tercel is blocking a row of pumps. The driver, a middle-aged woman in cargo shorts, a T-shirt, and army boots is yelling at me because I won't sell her a carton of cigarettes.

"Sorry," I say. "I can sell you two packs, but we're low and our cigarette shipment doesn't come in for three more days."

"This is fucked up," she says and sits in the doorway of the office.

"Ma'am, you need to move. You and your car are blocking customers."

There are two cars behind hers. There's a man on the other side of the door trying to get into the office.

"I don't give a shit," she says. "I'm not moving until you sell me a carton of Marlboros."

"We've already gone through this, ma'am."

"I'm having a bad day," she says. "I just want my cigarettes."

"Then buy a pack. Or two. I can't sell you a carton today. I'm sorry."

She screams. "I'm going to call the police," she says.

I grab the phone.

"Awesome idea," I say. "Let me call them for you."

I thought that would do it but she doesn't budge. So I dial. "Two squad cars are coming," I say when I hang up. "Your day is about to get worse."

She screams. "Fuckhead, Assfucker, Prick."

"You think you're having a bad day," I say. "Everybody has bad days. You're causing everyone here to have one as we speak."

She screams.

The cops show up. She kicks at their shins. One them gets behind her and slams her into the concrete. He cuffs her while the other reads her rights. The other cop asks me questions for twenty minutes. The waiting customers have left. People driving by the station crane their necks to see what is going on. I have to wait for a tow truck to come and take her car to the impound lot. By that time there's only an hour left of work.

PEACE

"I've made peace with it," I say and Cal asks with what. "My place in life. I accept that I am a college flunky. That's okay because I never thought college was for me anyway. It was just a way to move from A to B. And I accept that I may very well be working at a gas station for the rest of my life."

"You're breaking my heart," Cal says. "Don't be such a whiner."

"I'm not whining, I'm giving up. There's a difference. I think."

"We all go through shit," Cal says. He winks at me. "But not all of us get to be male prostitutes and porn stars."

I'll never live it down.

"The point is," Cal says, "that if you resign yourself to something then you have no choice, but if you make an effort there's no knowing the outcome."

"Are you telling me I can be whatever I want to be?"

"Shut up," he says.

"Thanks, Dad," I say and we both walk out to greet the customer pulling into the station.

MESSAGE #1

"It's me," Sarah says. "You're probably at work. Actually I know you're at work because I drove by the station about twenty minutes ago, but I didn't have the guts to come in. Even though I needed gas. I went to the station a couple blocks down the street from you instead. They were five cents higher than your station, but I didn't think I could stand to see you yet. It took three times dialing your number to finally let it ring. Two more to leave a message. You check your voicemail, right? You're not one of those people who just looks at their cell and sees who called, but ignores the message? I don't think you are. Maybe I'll try back. I don't know what to do. I think I still love you."

MESSAGE #2

"You're an asshole, did you know that? I can't believe I dated you. I can't believe I wanted you to meet my family. That I thought about how wonderful it would be for us to get married one day. You screwed up, because you are just like every other guy in the world. You're a fuckwad. You don't deserve me. You never did. All you do is pump gas, for God's sake. I don't even know what I was thinking. I must have been temporarily retarded. I'm over you. I just wanted you to know what a jerk you are."

MESSAGE #3

"It's me," Sarah says, almost whispering. "I'm sorry about the last message. I didn't mean it. I just don't know what to do with myself. Without you. I love you so much. It makes my stomach ache, like I'm going to throw up. I don't care about what you did. I mean, I care. But we can move past it. We can move on. I can. I want to be with you. I love you too much to let this be the end. I just wish that I could see you. That we could talk. I drive by the gas station every day and see you running around, working on cars, pumping gas, standing around laughing with your boss when it's slow. How can you goof around? Don't you miss me? I miss you so much. Please. Call me."

Raise

"You've been working hard," Cal says. "Really making a comeback. I put in a request for you to get a raise."

Another five cents an hour.

"Doesn't it seem useless?" I asked Craig once.

"This is the game," he said. "You get small raise here, a small raise there, a promotion, another raise. Next thing you know you're a manager, or doing a desk job."

That's what it all boils down to. There is always ladder to climb, even in the simplest jobs. I didn't realize it until I was apparently a couple of short rungs up it.

"Thanks," I say.

"You deserve it," Cal says. "And don't think I've stopped bugging them about letting us run the Quick Stop franchise." Cal is full of ideas. "We should open a service detailing cars," he says.

"Who would want to clean out someone else's car? I don't even clean out my own."

"We can make at least a hundred and fifty per car." Cal is forever unfazed.

This is when I realize it's not about the money so much as it is about not wanting to do certain jobs. I'd be happy with minimum wage if it was something I didn't hate doing.

COFFEE

I finally call Sarah back. She's filled my voicemail three times. Sent me text messages and even postcards and letters.

I tell her we can meet for coffee. She's already sitting with a cup in front of her when I get there. She has dark circles under her eyes. Her legs are crossed, one wags back and forth.

I order a tall black coffee and sit across from her. "You've got to stop with the phone calls and everything," I say.

"I've forgiven you for everything. Can't we put it behind us and get back together?"

"I don't think so."

"But I forgive you."

"You probably shouldn't."

"Why are you doing this to me?"

I tell her she needs a better person than me. "That girl I got pregnant was sixteen," I say.

She bites her lip and tells me that it's okay.

"No, it's not. I know that, but I don't know why I do things I know aren't right."

She tells me we'll figure it out together. I tell her we won't. I don't tell her that I hope to run into her one day when she's married and has three kids. I don't tell her that when she gets to that point she will be grateful I didn't take her back.

"I don't get it," she says. "I broke up with you, and now I want you back but you refuse. I don't understand."

"It's not supposed to make sense yet. But I think one day it will."

"I don't know what that means."

"You have to stop calling me. You have to stop sending me letters and notes. I'm sorry."

She's crying. Her forehead is pressed against the Formica table. Her arms are loose at her side. Everybody is looking at her. Us. I pour my coffee into a to-go cup and walk out the door. Even outside I can hear her.

PIZZA

My brother pulls into the station to fill up with Premium. I wash his windshield and he says he wants to take me to dinner. We agree on pizza and that six is a good time because it allows me to go home and shower first.

I get to the pizza place first and get us a table. He shows up ten minutes later. I'm already drinking my second beer. We order our food. Pepperoni for me and something with a myriad of vegetables for him.

"How are you doing?" he asks and I kick myself for not realizing there was an ulterior motive to this dinner.

"I'm fine," I say.

"You haven't been around much."

"I work. When I don't work I sit at home and try to relax."

"Mom and dad are worried about you."

"They shouldn't be."

"No offense," he says. "But you're looking like shit lately. What's with the beard and mohawk look?"

"Felt like something different."

The conversation continues until the pizzas come. I stuff my mouth to keep from talking. When the pizza is gone he orders us another round of beers.

"I know you're going through some shit," he says. "I'm your brother, I can tell. If you don't want to talk about it that's fine, but when you're ready to let me know." He downs the fresh beer and puts a credit card down on top of the bill.

When I'm getting in my car my brother is pulling out of the parking lot. He rolls down his window.

"Everybody cares about you," he says.

"What a world."

He drives away.

NEED

"You know what you need?" Cal asks, and I concede that I don't. "You need to go to a titty bar."

"Does anyone really need that?"

"Have you ever been?"

I tell him no.

"That's what you need. It takes your mind off things. It's relaxing."

"I'm not going to a strip joint. I'm not going to be that guy sitting alone at the bar getting drunk and wondering how to make the dancers fall in love with me."

"After work. You and me."

"You just want an excuse to go."

"It's Friday and you need to unwind."

"What about your wife?" I ask and he says she doesn't care.

"We go to Amsterdam every year," he says. "Stay at a hotel right next to all the hot spots so we can walk back when we get loaded."

We meet in the parking lot of a strip club in Medford.

"All right," Cal says. "Guys' night out."

There are only a few people inside. The girl on stage is topless. Probably in her mid-forties.

"The best girls don't come on until later," Cal says.

We sit at the bar and order drinks. The music drifts between butt rock and rap, depending on the dancer. No one strips to the Beatles. A few more people drift into the club. It's surprisingly dead for a Friday night. Even the bartender says so.

"I'm buying you a private dance," Cal says.

I refuse, but he doesn't listen. A blonde girl who doesn't look much older than eighteen or nineteen takes me by the hand. "I'm going to take you on a journey," she says and I try not to laugh. We go to a back room and she tells me to sit in a lounge chair between two partitions lined with red velvet.

"I'm not real comfortable with this," I say, and she tells me it'll be fine.

"Just enjoy yourself," she says.

"Do you enjoy yourself ?" I ask. I can't help myself.

She smiles. "I do," she says. She starts gyrating and slowly untying the blouse that is tied in a knot in front of her stomach. "Look, I know the stereotypes. But I don't have three kids at home, and I'm not pretending to work my way through med school." She drops the blouse. Runs her fingers across the mounds of cleavage presented by her black lace bra. "I don't expect to do this forever, but it's okay for now." She unhooks the bra. "Now have fun," she says and I nod.

When she's naked, except for fishnet stockings, she hovers over my lap. Her pubic hair is shaved into horizontal lines. "I've never seen that before," I say.

"Rumble strips," she says. "Like on the side of the freeway. I got the idea when I was driving to the mall."

She finishes dancing, stands in front of me, picking up the pieces of her outfit.

"How many men think they can convince you to come home with them?" I ask.

She turns, clutching bra and panties to her chest, one nipple peeking out. "All of them," she says. "If a customer doesn't think he's capable of getting me home he's not going to pay me to dance. I'd be a failure at my job."

BELIEFS

"I believe I might be the devil," I say wiping oil off my hands.

Cal throws a shop rag on the growing pile by the back door of the Quick Stop bay.

"I'm thinking about quitting," I say.

"Because you're the devil?"

"No. I just don't know what else to do."

"You're not quitting," he says.

I throw my rag on the pile. "You're right," I say. "But there's always the devil thing to deal with."

"Indeed," he says, which reminds me for some reason of watching the old BBC Sherlock Holmes movies with my mom when I was a kid.

Cal doesn't take me seriously. I don't always either. But some days I do and it worries me.

MAIL

There's a thick envelope in the mail. No return address, but I recognize Sarah's handwriting. There's no letter just a stack of photos.

The photos I took of her.

And at the bottom of the stack, the pictures she took of me. Close-ups of my beard. Pictures of my mohawk. And a picture of me sleeping I haven't seen before.

I check the back of each one for a note. Nothing.

Is she trying to rid herself of reminders of me? Is she trying to entice me with the naked pictures? Get me to call and ask her over? I toss the pictures of her into the trashcan under my sink. The pictures of me I pin up on the wall. They are the only things on my walls. The only pictures I have.

LOYALTY

"One day I'm going to quit," I say.

Cal rolls his eyes. "Is this going to be a daily thing with you?"

"I'm considering it."

"You're not going to quit. We're a team. We'll be running the whole company in a few years."

"People quit all the time," I say.

"Not you," Cal says. "You're too loyal to quit."

What Cal really thinks is that I have no other options. That I'm too sensible to quit a job with nothing else lined up.

But I saved nearly every dollar I made "whoring myself out" as Cal likes to put it. I have ten thousand dollars sitting in a bank account. Waiting.

"I'm just trying to prepare you," I say. "Because one day I won't be here anymore and you're not likely to find someone as awesome. I just want you to be ready."

DATE

Office Girl comes in for her cigarettes. "So," she says. "When are you going to ask me on a date?"

"I didn't know I was supposed to," I say.

"There are other places to buy cigarettes, you know."

I laugh.

"How about Friday night?" she asks.

"Sure," I say. "What time?"

We meet for dinner at eight. She's wearing a tight red dress that ends just after the bottom curve of her ass.

"You look spectacular," I say.

"You shaved off your mohawk."

"It was time. Plus I wasn't sure they'd let me in the restaurant."

"I liked it," she says.

She orders lobster. I have chicken parmesan. We split two bottles of Chardonnay.

"I can't believe you didn't have the stones to ask me out," she says, sliding her foot between my thighs.

"A gas station doesn't seem like the best place to ask a girl on a date."

She leans across the table "I can't wait to get you home."

I ask for the check.

I follow her home. Her house is in a nice neighborhood, on the hill above the library.

"I live alone," she'd said while we waited for the check.

The house is probably five times the size of my apartment. If not bigger. I can't imagine living in a place so big by myself. Once the front door is shut, she's on me. She digs her nails into my back, through my shirt. We go to her bedroom. I unzip the back of her dress and she shimmies out of it. She tells me to lie on the bed. She tells me to close my eyes.

I hear her open a drawer and pull something out. The drawer closes. I feel metal on my wrist. She's handcuffing me. I open my eyes and she's got a devilish grin stretched across her freckled face. She pulls off my pants.

"Hold on a second," she says and leans across the bed, lighting a candle on her bedside table. She straddles me. She picks up the candle and holds it over my chest.

I watch the wax fall onto my chest. It sears. I bite my tongue. "Fuck."

"Mmm," she says, starting to ride me.

The wax keeps dripping. "Jesus."

"Yes," she says.

Her eyes are closed. My skin feels like it's melting in little patches. As the wax dries it tugs on my chest hair. She rides harder. She arches backward and holds the candle over her own chest. I'm thankful for the reprieve.

She screams. "Yes," she says. "God." She rides harder. She drips wax on my stomach.

"Christ."

She pumps up and down. She pulls her own hair. Wax keeps dripping. "Yesyesyesgodyescome," she says. "fuckgodyes." She stops. Smiles. "Mmm."

I come. Out of relief for it being over. She kisses my stomach, chest, chin. She kisses my lips and runs her tongue over my teeth.

"Next time," she says. "I have something I'd like you to do to me."

JUMP

My car isn't starting. I call and tell Cal I'll be late. I call Craig and ask if he can give me a jump. I haven't talked to him since he came by my apartment to tell me he was quitting, but he says he'll be right over. I sit on the hood of my car until he shows up.

"You're lucky," he says. "I was in the middle of getting my asshole licked."

"You're sick," I say. "And we both know, if anything, you were spanking it."

He tosses me an end of the jumper cables and I hook them onto my battery. He hooks up his end and starts his truck. It takes a few turns of the ignition, but my car finally starts. Then the cables start smoking.

"Holy shit," Craig says.

The rubber grips on the connector handles are starting to melt.

"You got any gloves?"

"No," I say, popping my trunk.

There's an old towel that I don't remember ever putting in my trunk but it's been there almost since I bought the car. I wrap the towel around my hand and yank the connector from my car's battery. The heat burns through the towel. Melted rubber fuses to the cement of my driveway.

"I've never seen anything like that," I say.

"Me either," Craig says.

I kick the smoldering cables. "At least the jump worked."

POACHER

A truck pulls up with a Lube Stop logo on the door. I recall Cal saying his brothers own the Lube Stop franchise. A man in a suit gets out of the truck. It's clearly been a while since he's come close to changing oil.

"Howdy," he says. "I'm Frank."

"Cal's brother?" I ask and he nods. "Cal left early today."

"I know, I'm actually here to talk to you," Frank says. "Would you be interested in working for Lube Stop?"

"I'm not interested in changing oil in any capacity."

"Don't you change oil here?"

"Yes, but only because I'm already working here. Why would I take another job doing the same thing I'm already doing and hating?"

"From what Cal has said you're a sharp kid," Frank says. "How would you like to run a Lube Stop location?"

"So I can boss around other schmucks who make crap wages and hate their jobs and bosses? No thanks."

"You'd be on salary."

"I'd also be waking up too early, working too late, and be in charge of employees and a business I have no investment in."

"Cal must be an idiot," Frank says, turning and walking out the door. He slams his truck door and drives away.

MORE MAIL

Sarah has sent me more mail.

This time it's a padded manila envelope. Inside is a pair of red and black panties and a picture of man naked and asleep on her bed. His chest hair is so thick it looks like he's wearing carpet. He's balding and has a mustache.

Again there's no note.

Part of me wants to send her something. A picture of an oil filter perhaps. With a note that says, "Don't forget to have your oil changed every five thousand miles."

PLAN

"Your brother dropped by last week," I say and Cal looks up from his coffee.

"Which one?" he asks.

"Frank."

"What did he want?"

"To poach me. He offered me a job running a Lube Stop."

"What? The fucker. What did you tell him?"

"I said he was a capitalist pig and to leave me alone."

Cal laughs so hard a bit of coffee bubbles out of his mouth. "You didn't," he says.

"Close enough."

"You're an idiot."

"That's what he said about you. I guess we're really stuck."

Cal wipes his mouth and chin on his sleeve. "Jesus," he says. "What a brother."

"You shouldn't go bragging about how awesome I am then," I say and Cal tosses me an air filter that needs to be shelved.

"Maybe it was all part of my plan to get you out of my hair," he says.

ENGLISH MAJOR BLUES

It's seven o'clock. Two hours until closing. There hasn't been a customer since 5:45. I've been torturing myself since then. I think the last customer is to blame.

"How do you like working here?" she'd asked while I washed the windshield of her Nissan minivan.

"It's not bad," I said, because I knew she was just making chitchat and didn't really want me to examine my inner feelings about the job or some bullshit like that. But that's what I've been doing ever since she pulled out of the station.

I hate this job. I hate the town. I hate the stupid tourist season and the dead season, too. I hate the steady inflation of gas prices and the feeling of oil on my hands.

But what else is there for me? Get another job doing the same kind of shit? I couldn't even get a job washing dishes and I can't imagine liking that any better. Even when I was in college I didn't know why I was there. All my friends knew what they were going to be after school got out. They had majors that were conducive to real jobs. My friends were physics majors, pre-law, chemistry. Even psychology or physical therapy.

Me? I was an English major. Why? Because I like to read.

No one pays people to read. The only real option is teaching, but I'd suck at that. I couldn't teach a kid to tie his own shoe, let alone the meaning behind Emily Dickinson's crap poetry. And ultimately that leaves me here. Seven o'clock at night counting the cigarette inventory for the third time for something to do.

KINK

Office Girl comes in for her cigarettes.

"So," she says. "When are we going out again?"

She's got a wicked grin. I can't imagine what forms of torture she has left to translate to the realm of sex.

"I don't know," I say. It's the only thing I can make my mouth say.

"Well," she says. "You better give me call. You don't want me getting too hungry." She blows me a kiss and walks back across the street.

"What was that all about?" Cal asks.

"I think she's a government agent," I say.

"What?"

"That girl is schooled in forms of torture that only governments use. Only she tries to make them into porn."

"Kinky," he says.

"Yeah. Something like that."

DRUGGED

I get a hair up my ass and drive to Medford to go to a bar. I get one drink under my belt before I'm approached by a girl in faded jeans. She's got a nice rack. She sits next to me at the bar.

"Can I buy you a shot?" she asks.

"A girl buying a drink for a guy? Sure who could refuse," I say.

She orders two shots of tequila. I excuse myself to take a piss. When I'm walking back she's got her hand over the shot next to my empty glass. I don't think much of it, still stoked to have someone buying me a drink.

"Cheers," she says and watches me down the shot.

She says she has to go talk to her friends for a second and disappears to a table with five people around it. She comes back and makes small talk. I manage one more drink before I start feeling weird. Everything goes blurry, and I feel like I'm on a boat in the middle of a tidal wave.

I stand up. Nearly fall over.

I stumble toward the door and make it a couple steps outside. Three guys come out behind me.

"What the hell?" one of them says, but I can't respond.

"The girl just wanted to take you home," another says. "You should show a little class."

I try to stand up straight.

Before I get a chance one of the guys hits me. Then another. I'm on the ground and they get a few kicks to my ribs.

"Next time you'll be polite to a girl who just wants some company."

I want to say, "What the fuck?" But I cough instead. I want to say I wouldn't have had any problems going home with the girl. That despite the birthing hips she looked all right to me. But everything out of my throat is a gargle of blood and spit.

I wake up with my face pressed against the cold concrete. I can't see shit. Still feel like I'm on a boat. But I manage to crawl to my car and get inside. I sleep until morning. I have to get my face right next to the clock on my dashboard and squint real hard to make out the time.

I have to be at work in thirty minutes.

I drive back to Ashland, barely able to make out the road. I park behind the station and head into the office.

"Jesus," Cal says.

I tell him what happened, and he says, "Sounds like you got drugged."

I can't even read the pumps.

"You need to go home," Cal says and calls me a cab.

"Sleep that shit off," he says.

I walk across the station's lot to the cab. Each step is a game of trying to stay on my feet. Forget about trying to walk straight.

INSANITY

"I think this job is starting to drive me insane," I say.

Cal laughs.

"I'm serious. I need something different."

"Like what?"

"I don't know. That's the problem."

"Okay," Cal says. "I'll humor you. What's your ideal job?"

"A salary job with after noon hours so I don't have to wake up too early, but don't have to stay at work all night, either. And I'm the boss, so I can do things my way."

"Mmhmm. I hate to tell you this, but that job doesn't exist."

"I know."

"But if shit comes through and we get to run a chain of Quick Stops at least you would almost be your own boss and you would be on salary."

"I'd still be doing the same crap I am now, but with more responsibility."

"If you're going to be a boss you have to be okay with that part."

"Yeah, but I can't have more responsibility in a situation that drives me crazy."

"You're talking in circles now."

"You think this is bad," I say. "You should stick around for the conversations I have when I'm alone."

RUNAWAY

LILIJA

     The girl in the white Beetle looks familiar but I can't place it. I set the pump to fill and start washing her windshield.

     "Didn't we go to high school together?" she asks.

     That must be it.

     "I think so," I say.

     "Lilija," she says, the name sealing it.

     "Yeah," I say. "What are you up to these days?"

     "Just visiting family. I'm going to school in Portland. How about you?"

     "I was going to school outside of Portland, but I got kicked out."

     She laughs, showing a set of stark white teeth. "What did you do?" she asks and I tell her it's a long story. "Well," she says. "Maybe you should buy me dinner so I can hear it."

     The pump clicks off.

     "Sure," I say and she writes her cell number on the palm of my hand after signing her receipt.

FAST FOOD

Pulling into the Burger King parking lot I'm still suspicious of Lilija. That she's setting me up. What kind of girl wants to be taken to a fast food restaurant for dinner? But there she is, sitting in her car. The only one in the lot and she's bobbing her head. Hopefully to music, I think.

"Thanks for meeting me here," she says. "I hope you don't mind, my family's hardcore vegan. I don't think I ever want greasy fast food so much in my life as when I come home for visits."

"No problem. It's not every day a girl wants to eat at my favorite restaurant."

"So," she says, when we've picked a booth and are sitting across from each other, peeling our burgers out of their wrappers, "let's hear that story."

I try to tell the whole thing in the most positive way I can. Making myself seem less irresponsible and more like a goof who maybe took it a step too far. She laughs the whole time, intermittently making me stop so she can chew without choking.

When I finish the story she says, "You're an idiot. And I mean that in the best way possible."

"What are you going to school for?"

"Psychology."

"I've known a few of you. You're analyzing me right now, aren't you?"

"Only a little," she says, reaching across my tray to steal a couple of French fries. "But don't let it worry you."

MIDNIGHT

It's midnight. I'm laying on my futon in my underwear, watching late night TV. My phone rings. I break out in a momentary cold sweat. Is it Sarah? Olivia? Sondra? I get up and grab my phone from the kitchen counter.

It's Lilija.

"Hello," I say, trying not to sound hurried or panicked.

"Hey," she says. "Sorry for calling so late, but everybody in my family is a freak and goes to bed insanely early."

"It's cool." I must sound stupid. "I was just watching TV."

"God, I wish," she says. "My mom went on a righteous kick a few years ago and threw our TV out."

"Lame."

"You're not kidding."

"Well you're welcome to come stare at mine. TV that is. My TV."

She laughs. "Really?"

"Yeah. I'll even throw on some pants so you won't feel awkward."

"Or I could take mine off."

"Whatever works," I say and she says she'll be right over.

I call her back and tell her where I live.

PROPOSITION

It takes fifteen minutes before Lilija knocks on my door.

"You put on pants," she says.

"So did you."

"I always forget how brutal it is to be home. I can't believe I lived there for eighteen years."

"I moved out the summer before our senior year."

"I think I remember that," she says. "It's weird that we went to high school together, but never talked until now."

"It's understandable," I say. "You weren't ready to deal with my awesomeness."

"That must be it."

I tell her to make herself comfortable and she sinks into the couch. I pour myself a whiskey sour and ask her if she wants anything.

"Whatever you're having," she says. "Thanks for having me over."

"It's the best scenery this apartment's had in a long time," I say.

She raises her eyebrows, then gives me what I think is a wink, but it looks more like a twitch.

We watch TV until three.

"I hope you don't have to work tomorrow," she says and I tell her I do. "I should get some sleep," she says, nestling her head into my shoulder.

"You can crash here," I say and she looks up at me. "Are you propositioning me?"

"Only if you want me to."

"That sounds nice," she says, reclining and pulling me on top of her.

DISTRACTION

I burn my hand on an engine block. I mis-thread two oil filters. I over-pump two tanks.

"You're having quite a day," Cal says.

All I can think about is Lilija. And not just her milk-white naked body, or perfect handful breasts. Her laugh keeps playing in my head. Her voice and smirky half-smile.

Truth is I remember her from high school. Better than she probably remembers me. I had a crush on her from the first day of freshman year. I had dreams about her. I almost asked her out a handful of times, but always lost my nerve at the last second and said stupid things like, "having fun yet?" as we walked out of our economics class.

Truth is I've wanted her for years, so it's only natural that I can't get her out of my head. That when I close my eyes I can feel her body pressed against me. Right?

"Don't worry," she'd said just as I was about to cum. "I'll never analyze you when we're fucking." Then she burst out laughing and I was laughing, too, but still came.

"That was priceless," she said. She apologized and said she couldn't help it and we both laughed more.

The pump clicks off and I realize I've washed the customer's windshield three times.

"Thanks for the thorough job," the man says as he signs his receipt.

"There was some gunk," I say and he nods.

Lilija was still sleeping when I left for work. I wrote her a note and told her to stay as long as she liked, just to lock the door on her way out.

I almost wrote, "I'll be back at nine if you're still around." But that would have been too transparent. Too needy and desperate. Still, I spend the first few hours of the day hoping she'll be there when I get home, wrapped up in my blanket killing time watching TV.

Then she comes in for gas. "Hey hot thing," she says. "Thought I'd see how good you are at your job." I set the pump running and wash her windshield. "You're cute when you're laboring," she says laughing.

"You going back to your house?"

"Hell no," she says. "I'm going to lunch and then I'm going to bum around town until you get off work."

"Oh really?"

"Yep, because then you are going to buy me a late dinner and take me home to do unspeakable things."

"If you say so."

I watch her drive off, trying not to be obvious about it.

"So," Cal says. "That's what turned you into an idiot today."

TOP FIVE

We curl up in front of the TV with frozen lasagna cooking in the oven. "What are your five favorite songs?" I ask and Lilija takes a deep breath.

"That's a tough one, Oprah," she says.

The timer rings and I hop up to get our dinner.

"Okay," she says, following me. "'Day Tripper,' 'Lay Lady Lay,' 'Punk Rock Girl' by The Dead Milkmen, 'Mother' by Danzig and 'UMass' by the Pixies."

Fuck.

"Nice list," I say. "In fact you're even hotter now."

"Oh really," she says leaning over my shoulder and kissing my cheek.

"I have a theory that no relationship can work if the people hate each other's music."

"I could buy into that. I guess I need to know your top five then."

"'Long Long Long,' 'Cocaine Blues,' 'Skulls,' 'Where Is My Mind?' and also 'Lay Lady Lay.'"

"You're not just saying that because I picked it?"

"Nope, my mom used to listen to Dylan when I was a kid. It got engrained in me." I hand her a plate of lasagna and we head back to the couch.

"Now we just need to get tattooed together," she says.

"Awesome, let's do it."

"Really?"

"Yeah," I say. "I'll call the guy who did my last one and see if he can get us in next weekend."

"Sweet," she says, scooting closer to me. "I'd kiss you, but I've got lasagna mouth."

"My favorite kind," I say, leaning over her plate.

TWINS

Davis gets us in for back-to-back appointments. He's licensed now and working at a legitimate parlor.

"Been a while," he says when we walk in.

"They work me too hard," I say.

"Who's going first?" he asks and I point to Lilija.

She's getting a hummingbird. She was going to get it on her thigh, but I said I couldn't watch a guy play with her leg, so she's getting it on her arm.

She has three other tattoos. A line of stars up the back of her left calf, a crow on her right shoulder blade, and a stack of books with a little girl sitting on top on her upper left arm. She rolls up her sleeve and grins nervously, her forehead already beginning to bead with sweat as Davis sets up his ink and gun.

Her eyes are locked with mine the whole time. Just over an hour. I make faces at her, give her thumbs up, make goggles with my forefingers and thumbs and peer through them at her. Her look doesn't change, just stares with a half-grin plastered on her face.

Then it's my turn. I give Davis a picture. Bernard, the blue wild thing from *Where the Wild Things Are*.

"Nice," he says, placing the traced version of it on my left forearm.

My eyes wander back and forth between the needle running in and out of my skin, Lilija who is beaming and winking at me, and Davis wiping the excess ink away with a dampened paper towel.

Nerves burn. I smile at Lilija, my teeth gripped together. When it's done I pay Davis for both tattoos, and Lilija kisses my cheek, holding her arm awkwardly out to the side. When we're walking up the street Lilija says, "Now we're ink twins."

"As long as we're not any other kind of twins," I say.

ROOMMATE

Without thinking about it I invited Lilija to stay with me for the summer. "Then you won't have to deal with your family as much," I'd said.

"Really? You're sure?"

I told her I was. And that was the weird part. I was sure.

So, she brought two suitcases to my apartment and placed her toothbrush next to mine.

"My parents hate you already," she said gleefully.

She was working at a bar downtown during the day and we spent our nights making frozen dinners, watching TV, and screwing like wild animals trying to keep their species off the endangered list.

Cal makes fun of me for becoming a married man overnight and I tell him I'm having more sex than he and his wife have had over the last decade. The crap-flinging stops.

"This is only for the summer," Lilija assures me. "I have to go become a shrink, you know." She is full of warnings. "I've had a crazy life."

"You grew up in Ashland, Oregon," I say. "Same place as me. You can't have had that crazy of a life."

But I'm wrong and she proves it. Tells me about the six months she spent living with hippies in a park in Seattle after running away from home. She was thirteen. She tells me about the anorexia and the meth. "But don't worry," she says. "My only vices now are liquor and your cock."

And through all of it I find her only more endearing. "We've all done shit," I say and she makes me promise to tell her my stories one night. "I'll put that off as long as possible, thank you very much."

We drink and peel each other out of our clothes. "I like the way you smell," she says. "That mix of gasoline and Old Spice. Just like fucking heaven."

And though I don't say it, I recognize this as the moment when I've completely lost my mind and fallen in love.

SOCIOPATH

Lilija and I sit on the couch and read the letter together. It's from Sarah. "I've noticed there's a whore living with you now," is how it starts. I keep one eye on Lilija to gauge her reaction. She nearly falls off the couch laughing by the end of the letter.

"Jesus," she says. "What kind of girls did you date before me."

"That's what I'm always telling you," I say. "You think you're crazy, but you're the least crazy girl I've ever been with."

"That's some serious stalker shit."

"The last one had a pair of panties in it."

"No way," she says. "What did you do with them?"

"Threw them away. I'm not that perverted."

Lilija's eyes light up. "You should let me call her."

I laugh. "Yeah right. I keep hoping she'll get the point and leave me alone."

"Maybe she's a sociopath. We learned a lot about them in school. What if she ends up killing you?"

"I'll use you as a shield."

Lilija hits me on the shoulder. "I knew you were a rat," she says and then we're rolling on the floor, Sarah's letter getting crumpled under our bodies.

COMPLAINT DEPARTMENT

It started as a trickle. A small leak. "I got a complaint about you this morning," Cal says when I punch in my time card. "A woman said you were rude and inconsiderate."

I feel the blood drain from my cheeks. "Was it Sarah?" I ask.

He says, "No, it was woman named Catherine."

They all come back. One way or another. Sondra had, Sarah was still doing it, and now Catherine.

"I haven't seen Catherine in the station in months," I say.

"Why the complaint then?"

"Look, she's one of the women I used to sleep with. I stopped answering her phone calls a while back."

But then the trickle became a river. Then small leak a bursting dam. Soon Cal was fielding complaints like he was a hotline for that sole purpose. "A woman today said you sexually harassed her," he says. Then three separate women were complaining I had sexually harassed them.

"I'm starting to think they're holding meetings or something," I say.

"Even Office Girl turned on you," he says.

"God, it's like the Salem witch trials or something."

One of the suits shows up at the station to talk to me. "Let's take a walk," he says, so we walk through the neighborhood behind the station. "We want to stand by you," he says. "You've been a loyal employee and Cal says you're the hardest worker he's got. But you need to tell me where all this is coming from."

I spill it all. Leaving out the part that I was fucking them for money, I tell him about sleeping with married women and customers.

"Basically you need to learn to keep it in your pants," he says.

I nod, try to laugh.

"Look," he says. "Whatever you do don't talk to any of these women on your own. Let the company handle it."

I tell him I have no desire to talk to any of them. And I wonder how much they think I care about my job pumping gas to try and get me fired. I won't exactly be heartbroken, I think, and when I get back to the office Cal says it's best if I take the rest of the day off.

VISITATION

I stop in the bar where Lilija works.

"To what do I owe this unexpected visit?" she asks, and I tell her they gave me the rest of the day off.

"There's some shit going down," I say and of course she wants to know. "I'll explain later."

She pours me a whiskey. The bar is empty. I lean across the counter and whisper in her ear, just to watch her cheeks flush.

She snaps a washrag at me. "Down boy."

I tell her I'll see her at home and she winks.

COMING CLEAN

"There's a lot to tell," I say.

"Don't worry I won't judge you much." She laughs and urges me onward.

After telling everything to the suit, I figured there wouldn't be a better time to get it all out there on the table with Lilija. So, I tell her everything. I don't leave anything out.

I tell her I had sex for money and she says, "That's awesome."

I tell her about Olivia and she says, "That sucks."

I tell her I think I might be the devil. She scoffs.

"You've done some stupid shit," she says. "Some funny shit.

But it's all about what you take from it I guess." She kisses my forehead. "None of that has anything to do with us," she says. "That's all that matters."

And I say them. Those three words I dread, that I barely even use with my parents. "I love you," I say.

She says it back, then, "Fuck that's crazy." She laughs. "Sorry, I just didn't expect to fall for some guy over summer break.

"I hear you," I say.

"You're not on summer break."

"Smart ass."

ROUTINE

There are only three and a half weeks before Lilija has to leave for school. She hasn't said much about it, but I remember the date from a conversation the first time we went to dinner.

I don't bring it up either.

We've settled into a routine, meeting each other at home after work, making dinner and drinking. Watching TV or movies. Putting on Pixies albums and fucking over every inch of the apartment. I try to imagine what it will be like when she goes back to school and I can't picture it. Can't imagine what it will be like to come home and drink all night by myself. Just a couple months ago I wouldn't have been able to imagine anything but that.

"I would do stupid shit for you," I say and Lilija gives me a sixty-watt smile.

"Right back at you, Chief," she says.

STALKER

Sarah shows up at the apartment on a Saturday. Lilija points her out. "There's a girl sitting in a car looking up here," she says and I look out the window.

"It's the sociopath," I say.

"You should call the police," Lilija says, but I tell her I can handle it.

I go outside and Sarah rolls down her window. "Who's the slut?"

"You've got to let it go," I say and she's already sobbing. Not to mention slamming her forehead against the steering wheel. "Come on," I say. "You've got to move on."

"I love you."

"But I don't love you."

"Do you love her?"

"Yes, I do."

"Fuck you," she says.

"You need to leave me alone," I say. "I don't want to get a restraining order, but I will if you don't stop."

She flips me off and rolls up her window. She guns her engine and peels out, leaving tire marks for five feet down the road.

SENSITIVITY

The suit is back at the station. "I've talked to all the women who have complained. None of them are filing any sort of lawsuit. You've really dodged a bullet this time," he says. "But the company wants to make sure we don't have any problems in the future, so we'd like you to go to a sensitivity training course."

I agree to go. The suit slaps me on the back.

"You're going to be all right," he says. Then he gets in his white truck drives away.

"Sensitivity training," Cal says. "That sucks." He's grinning like an idiot.

"Be careful," I say, "or I'll tell them we could all benefit from it."

"I'm sure you'll have fun."

"I'm not going."

"You have to."

"Not if I quit."

"Bullshit," Cal says. "I call bullshit."

CELEBRATION

I don't tell Lilija what I'm thinking about. Just that all the complaints have been dropped and she says, "We should celebrate." So we go out to dinner.

"I can't believe I have to go back to school," she says.

"I've been trying not to bring it up."

She puts her hand on mine. "We'll figure something out."

"We better," I say. "I haven't been putting in all this time for nothing.

When we finish dinner we go out for ice cream and walk through downtown. It's still eighty degrees out, but there's a breeze that makes it nicer than it should be. We walk through the park.

"We should do something crazy," she says. "Have you ever had sex outdoors?"

I say, "No" and she takes off running up the path through the park. I take off after her. We pass the three duck ponds and come to a nice clearing of grass. She collapses on her back. I pretend to lunge at her, diving into the grass, landing at her side.

"Want to do it?" she asks, her mouth right next to my ear, tickling my spine.

I nod and she reaches down to unzip my pants. The grass is cool against my neck as Lilija straddles me, her pants lying next to my head.

"Someone might see," I say, and she kisses my chest.

"Let them have their free entertainment," she says.

I grab her shoulders and turn, getting on top.

"Let's howl at the moon," she says.

I tell her that's what I'm aiming for.

NOTICE

"I'm giving my two weeks," I say.

Cal doesn't look up from the engine he's hunched over, checking the oil. "We back on that?" he says, and I tell him I'm not kidding.

"Two weeks notice," I say. "Then I'm out like bell bottoms."

"You find another job?"

"No, I'm moving."

"Where?"

"Portland."

"Is this for that girl?" he asks.

I nod. "But also because I can't stand this place anymore. I didn't want to end up back here."

"You don't know what you're doing," Cal says, spitting. "You have no idea what you're doing."

"Come on," I say. "You didn't expect me to work here forever did you?"

"I expected us to run this company in another year or two."

"But I don't want to run this company. If I could never see a gas station again in my life that would be okay by me."

"You're just running away," he says. "Running away because you think there's something better, rather than making the best of what you have."

"That's the difference between settling for something or not," I say. "I might not ever have better than this, but at least I'm willing to find out."

"Fuck."

"This has nothing to do with anything but wanting to do something different. This isn't a personal thing."

"I know," he says. "I'm going to take off early, can you handle things?" He pulls his keys from his pocket and walks to his car.

"See you tomorrow," I say and he slams his door.

BREAKING THE NEWS

"I quit today," I say and Lilija stands from the couch and faces me in the kitchen. "What?"

"Gave my two weeks."

"Holy shit. Why?"

"Well, I didn't want to tell you yet, but I'm moving."

Her face muscles melt, her cheeks falling, lips gaping slightly. "Where?"

"I was thinking Portland."

She jumps into my arms. "Really?"

"Yeah."

She kisses me. "Awesome. That's awesome. This is going to be great."

"Another thing to celebrate," I say, grinning so big it makes my face hurt.

"You bet," she says pushing me against the refrigerator.

THE HAPPENING

It happens. It had never happened before, but it happens this time and I'm leaning over Lilija dripping sweat and panting like a dog.

"What happened?" she asks and I shake my head.

"So," I say, the only word I can get out between breaths.

"It'll come back," she says. "You just wore yourself out. Give it a minute."

So, I stick it out. Hold myself up, inches above her body shining with sweat. We kiss. I grope her breasts. Nothing happens.

"Fuck."

I slump next to her on the blanket, which is spread out on the floor. "

It's okay," she says. "It happens. Doesn't mean it's going to keep happening."

"Better not."

"Probably nerves," she says. "It's a big thing to quit your job, not to mention picking up and moving."

"There's nothing I want more than to get out of here. To be wherever you are."

"It's still hard to do."

"At least something's hard," I say and she kisses me.

"It'll be back," she says and pulls the blanket around us like a burrito.

LAST WEEK

The words feel great coming out of my mouth.

"This is my last week."

The station's regular customers have a variety of responses. "That sucks, who am I going to tell dirty jokes to?" or "That's great, good luck." Even, "I'm glad you're not getting sucked into this pit."

Cal is barely talking to me. Then one of the suits shows up.

"I hear you're leaving us," he says.

"Yep," I say, not even trying to hide my smile.

"What can I do to keep you here?" he asks and I tell him nothing could keep me here. "What if we give you a station to run? We've got one on the coast that needs a new manager. We could set you up there, you could live by the ocean."

"I don't want to live by the ocean."

"How much money would you need to make to stay?"

"It's not about money."

"It's always about money."

"Not this time," I say.

He shakes his head. "You going back to school?"

"I don't know what I'm doing yet."

He leans on the hood of his truck. "And there's nothing we can do to keep you? We don't want to lose an employee like you."

"Sorry," I say and he shakes my hand.

"Well, I had to try," he says.

"Man," Cal says. "When you blow it you blow it big."

VINDICATION

When I get home the lights are off and Lilija has lit a few candles. The couch is pulled out into a bed and she's sitting there in pink and black lingerie.

"Like?" she asks.

"Of course," I say, reaching for her hand and pulling her to her feet.

"I thought maybe we should do things right," she says.

I kiss her neck. Chest. Arms, hands, and the patch of stomach that is exposed.

"Seems a shame to take it off after five minutes," she says, grinning.

"Actually I think that's its expiration period," I say, peeling a strap off her shoulder.

And everything goes right. I pull the lingerie over her head, unsnap her bra, slide her panties down her legs.

Thoughts pop into my head. Can I keep it up? Will I go limp?

I push them aside and focus on Lilija's body. Her face. The way she bites her bottom lip when I hit it just right.

It works and she smiles at me. Opens her eyes.

"Told you," she says.

And I say, "Don't get too cocky yet, we're doing this all night."

GOODBYE

My last day at the gas station.

I'm surprised how many customers come in just to see me off. The college's mail van driver even brings a going away card. Dirty joke guy and his wife bring me cookies.

At 4:50pm a car pulls up for an oil change and Cal says, "We can tell them we're closing."

I shake my head. "Let's rock one more oil change, boss." The corners of his smile disappear into his mustache.

While oil drains, I say a silent prayer for it to be the last time I ever have to work under a car. With a car at all for that matter. If there's a God any further relationships I have with cars will be strictly recreational.

Cal hangs out until closing, then asks if I want to get a beer.

With cool, sweating bottles in our hands he says, "Here's to something more," and we clink bottlenecks. We don't say anything else until we've finished four rounds and he pats me on the back and says, "Well, we'll be seeing you" and walks out of the bar. I turn to pay the bartender but he waves a couple twenties at me and says Cal already did.

"Any time I see fleece I'll think of you," I say, even though Cal is probably starting his car by now.

LEAVING

So, both our cars are filled to the max and we're standing in my empty apartment. Everything is settled. We'll drive to Portland and I'll get a hotel room until I can find an apartment. School doesn't start for a few days for Lilija and in the meantime she'll investigate if she can get out of her campus housing.

"I'm so excited," she says.

I smile and kiss her forehead. Hold her close to my chest. "You ready to hit the road?"

"Are you?"

I close the door and lock it. Drop my keys in the mailbox like my landlord instructed.

"I need gas," Lilija says.

"Me, too."

"Your station?" she asks, laughing a little like it's an inside joke.

"No," I say. "Follow me."

GAS

Craig is there, hustling around the pumps like they're backed up, though there's only one car there when Lilija and I pull in.

"Holy shit," he says. "What's this all about?"

"I'm moving," I say, then I get out of my car and introduce him to Lilija.

"Shit," he says. "Seems like just yesterday you were a baby." He laughs and snorts. "Man, this town won't be the same."

"Don't worry," I say. "You can still call and leave me drunken messages."

"Who me?"

He fills our tanks and even takes the squeegee from my hand and washes our windshields.

"You're done with this shit," he says. "So what the hell are you going to do with yourself?"

"I don't know," I say, wrapping my arms around Lilija. "We'll be John and Yoko, Sid and Nancy, Bonnie and Clyde. Whatever. It doesn't matter. We can have a traveling puppet show for special kids for all I care."

Lilija leans her head back and kisses my chin, then rubs her lips for a second in my beard.

"Should've given me some warning," Craig says. "I'd have bought you a beer or something." He slaps me on the back. "Get on the road. And don't stop."

Lilija gets in her car. We already agreed to try and follow one another on I-5. I kiss her through the window.

"See you at a rest stop," she says.

"See you in my rear-view mirror." I get in my car and salute Craig.

"I don't want to see your ugly face back here," he says.

I tell him not to worry, then I start my car and pull onto the road out of town.

1–5
[PARALLEL OR TOGETHER]

The freeway stretches out before me like the goddamn road to paradise. I watch Lilija in my rear-view mirror.

I wait for panic to set in, but it doesn't and I realize I've never been so peaceful about a decision in my life. I don't even bother thinking about all the choices I have to make. Do I go back to school? Can I get a job that doesn't require the phrase, "What can I do for you?" or any like it? All that shit has faded like the sound of my car beneath speakers pounding out song after song.

Lilija sends me a text message saying she wants to stop at the next rest area, so we pull off the freeway outside of Salem. An hour away from my new home and the next chapter of my fuck-up life. Maybe the one where I start getting things right.

We hold hands as we walk to the bathrooms. Something I would have found sappy and ridiculous a few months ago, but is suddenly necessary. Vital even.

She meets me back at the cars, wraps her arms around my waist and we kiss.

"What are you listening to?"

"Ted Leo and the Pharmacists," she says.

"No shit? *The Tyranny of Distance*?"

"Yep."

"Holy fuck, me too," I say and she doesn't believe me at first. "I'm not kidding," I say. "It's a perfect driving album."

She smiles.

"This," I say, "is how I know we are meant to be together."

She kisses me again before we get back in our cars.

"See you in Portland," she says.

We pull out of the rest stop and I let her go ahead of me. We merge back onto I-5. I see Lilija looking in her rear-view mirror and I blow her a kiss. At that moment, I realize there is nothing behind me, nothing to return to. Not as far as I'm concerned. Everything that matters is ahead.

I had a dream the night before we left that our story never ended, but gas prices kept rising.

ACKNOWLEDGMENTS

To my bosses at the gas station, Chris and Kevin, who managed to make being a pump jockey tolerable.

Though I didn't talk about this project during my MFA, thanks to the writers who mentored me, especially Pete Fromm and Jack Driscoll without whose influence I would be much less of a writer.

To Rose Hunter for reading this manuscript before nearly anyone else and saying nice things. Ben Tanzer, Kyle Minor, Gary Amdahl, and Paul Di Filippo for being inspirations and friends. Jason Jordan at *decomP* for publishing an excerpt from the book.

To Scott Rogers and Black Coffee Press for believing in a story about a screw-up gas station attendant written by a former screw-up gas station attendant.

To John Dermot Woods for being a friend and supporter, and for being kind enough to whip up an illustration to fulfill a vision for the look of this book.

To my parents, who encouraged my love of writing from the beginning: well, this is what you get.

To my sons, River and Lincoln. If you read this book one day, I'm sorry.

Most of all to my beautiful and loving wife, Lisa, who loved my writing before she loved me. Which means she knew what she was getting herself into and still took the leap. I couldn't be more grateful.

RYAN W. BRADLEY has fronted a punk band, done construction in the Arctic Circle, and managed an independent children's bookstore. He is now a shipping and receiving co-ordinator at a university bookstore and a freelance book designer. He is the author of three chapbooks, *Aquarium* (Thunderclap Press, 2010), *Love and Rod McKuen* (Mondo Bummer, 2011), and *Mile Zero* (Maverick Duck Press, 2011), and a story collection, *Prize Winners* (Artistically Declined Press, 2011). *Code for Failure* is his first novel. He received his MFA from Pacific University and lives in Oregon with his wife and two sons.

12421204R00138

Made in the USA
Charleston, SC
04 May 2012